ENTOMBED

BRIAN KEENE

deadite
press

DEADITE PRESS
205 NE BRYANT
PORTLAND, OR 97211
www.DEADITEPRESS.com

AN ERASERHEAD PRESS COMPANY
www.ERASERHEADPRESS.com

ISBN: 1-62105-049-1

Acknowledgements

This time around, my thanks and sincere appreciation go to everyone at Deadite Press, Tony and Kim at Camelot Books, Mark Sylva, Tod Clark, Mary SanGiovanni, and my sons. Special thanks to Andy Deane, Bella Morte, and Metropolis Records for their kind permission to use the lyrics of "The End of the End". Please give them your support.

DEADITE PRESS BOOKS BY BRIAN KEENE

Urban Gothic
Jack's Magic Beans
Take The Long Way Home
A Gathering of Crows
Darkness On the Edge of Town
Tequila's Sunrise
Dead Sea
Kill Whitey
Castaways
Ghoul
The Cage
Dark Hollow
An Occurrence In Crazy Bear Valley
Entombed
Ghost Walk
Clickers II (with J. F. Gonzalez)
Clickers III (with J. F. Gonzalez – ebook only)

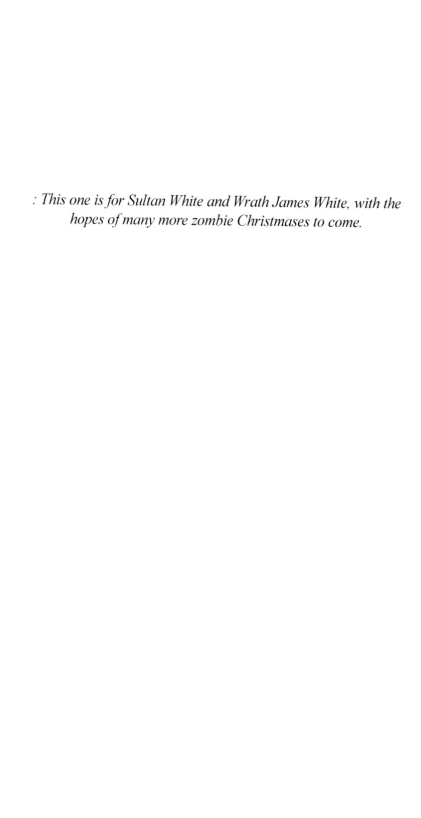

: This one is for Sultan White and Wrath James White, with the hopes of many more zombie Christmases to come.

Author's Note

This novel takes place in the same "reality" as my novel Dead Sea, however, since it is not a direct sequel, knowledge of one isn't required to enjoy the other. Also, although many of the locations in this novel are based on real places, I have taken certain fictional liberties with them. I've also fictionalized other locations based upon a variety of their real-life counterparts. So if you live in any of them, don't look for your favorite luxury hotel or impregnable nuclear war bunker. You won't like what's lurking there now.

ONE

I was sitting in the movie room, watching an episode of *Aqua Teen Hunger Force* for the twentieth time and talking to the disembodied head of Dwight D. Eisenhower, when the rest of the group decided that we should all start eating each other.

Pickings were slim for my viewing pleasure. The bunker's media collection consisted of a season of Reba McEntire's old sitcom, an episode of *The Wiggles*, a couple of Will Ferrell movies, the re-mastered and updated first *Star Wars* trilogy, a season of *Aqua Teen Hunger Force*, a season of *American Idol*, and a documentary about deer hunting. I avoided watching *Reba* because seeing Joanna Garcia, the actress who played Reba McEntire's daughter, made me horny, and that was a totally unhelpful feeling to have when one is sixty feet under the ground and recently divorced. Ditto *The Wiggles* (say what you will, but some of their dancers were totally fucking hot). Watching the deer hunting documentary made me think about how much I missed deer bologna and venison steaks, and that made me hungry—which was an even less helpful feeling down here in the bunker than being horny. I'd watched *Star Wars* a few times since we came down here, but it still pissed me off that in this updated version of the film, Han Solo no longer shot Greedo first. And as for Will Ferrell? Fuck him. I never liked Will Ferrell's movies—he was about as funny as cancer. And I'd thought that *American Idol* sucked even before the world ended, and saw no reason to start watching it now. Besides, it didn't matter who won, since they were probably all dead now.

That left *Aqua Teen Hunger Force*, which was okay with me, although sometimes I wished that someone would have left some *Metalocalypse* DVDs down here, too. Sometimes I wondered if the guys who'd created those shows were still alive somewhere, maybe sequestered in a bunker like I was and still making shows in the hopes that someone might see them some day.

I had the lights turned off. The media room was lit only by the glow from the huge flat-screen television that occupied most of the wall at the front of the room. I was sitting in the left hand side of the front row, right next to Eisenhower's head. The chairs weren't very comfortable. They hurt my butt if I sat in them too long, and they squeaked every time I moved around. Before Hamelin's Revenge turned the world to shit, the chairs had only been used by visitors to the bunker—tourists who sat in them once a day to watch a seven-minute documentary on the facility's history. Dwight D. Eisenhower was a big part of that history, which was why his head was in the movie room, too. That was also why the movie room had been updated to play DVDs rather than the old reel-to-reel movies. It was easier for me and my fellow tour guides to press play on a DVD player than to fool around with actual film canisters. I thought Eisenhower would have approved.

Eisenhower didn't say much. He couldn't. He was a bronze bust, and bronze busts don't talk. But that was okay with me. He didn't have to say anything. He was a good listener, and a good listener was what I needed—especially since most of the other people down here were slowly turning bat-shit crazy. There was more than one Eisenhower in the room. Framed pictures of him hung on the walls, along with photographs of the hotel sitting above the bunker, and a few snapshots of the facility from when it was still under construction—old black and white images of the Army Corps of Engineers swarming over the site with bulldozers and dump trucks and cranes.

Swarming, just like the dead rats that swarmed out of the sewers in New York City. That was how this whole thing started—Hamelin's Revenge. New York seems so far away, especially here in the mountains of West Virginia. But it must be true what they say—that New York City is the center of the world, because what started there swept across the rest of the planet in less than a month's time. I still get chills when I imagine what it must have been like. It happened during the evening rush hour. Zombie rats crawled out of the sewer and began attacking pedestrians. Being dead, they moved much slower than a living rat would, but that didn't matter. The city was so choked with traffic that their pickings were easy. The sidewalks and streets and bus stops and subway platforms were gridlocked, packed with commuters. People tried to get away but there was nowhere to go. The rats fed. Many people were bitten to death, the flesh stripped from their faces and hands, their stomachs chewed open so that their attackers could get to the good stuff inside. Many more victims were trampled to death as their fellow New Yorkers fled.

The breaking news dominated television and the internet that night. At first, MSNBC called it a riot, and both CNN and FOX speculated that it had been a possible terrorist attack. Soon, they confirmed that it had been rats—dead rats. As impossible as that sounded, eyewitness accounts confirmed that the rats were indeed dead when they began their attack. Pundits scoffed at this, and the authorities refused to comment, but soon enough, the live footage proved this to be true, as unlikely as it seemed. The coverage was fluid and the situation on the ground grew more chaotic with each passing hour. FOX had footage from inside a hospital. The emergency room was filled with wounded New Yorkers. Those who had suffered bites got sick very quickly. A short time later, they died. And after they died, they came back, just like the rats.

Before that first night was through, the media already had a name for it—Hamelin's Revenge, the return of the rats the pied piper was hired to get rid of. It didn't seem to matter that Hamelin was the name of the town, rather than the piper himself. I don't know. I used to wonder sometimes if the media had names and graphics on standby, just waiting to use them when all hell broke loose. It certainly seemed that way that night. There was Wolf Blitzer on TV, with a big graphic of a pied piper dressed like the Grim Reaper standing behind him and the words 'Hamelin's Revenge' superimposed over the character. Dead people and dead rats attacked the living, and then those who'd been infected joined their ranks. The media referred to the dead as cannibals, but then, during a 2am news conference, the White House Press Secretary used the word that was on everyone's mind.

Zombies.

By dawn the next morning, the National Guard had locked everything down. New York City was officially quarantined. They blockaded the bridges and tunnels and rail tracks. The Guardsmen were given the order to fire on anyone trying to escape the city, and some of them actually did. They gunned down civilians in cold blood. Then some of the other soldiers refused the order to shoot civilians and turned on their comrades instead. Soon enough, the troops were fighting each other—and fighting the civilians who shot back, as well. While dissent broke out in the military ranks, Hamelin's Revenge broke out of the city. It showed up in Newark, then Trenton, and then Philadelphia. By the end of the second day, it had spread to Buffalo, Baltimore, Washington D.C. and over the border into parts of Canada. The President declared martial law nationwide, even in those areas where the disease hadn't shown up yet. The army was mobilized. But by then, it was too late. You could shoot a zombie but you couldn't shoot the disease that caused it to get up and walk around in the first place. All it took was one bite, one drop of blood, pus from an open sore or cut—any exposure to infected bodily fluid— and you became one of them. People that died normal deaths, from illness or accidents or murder, stayed dead, but those who came into direct contact with the disease and managed to get infected—they became zombies. At first, the disease only infected humans, rats and mice. By the second week, however, it had jumped species and started showing up in dogs, cats, cattle, bears, coyotes, goats, sheep, monkeys and other animals. Some creatures, like pigs and birds, seemed to be immune, but most weren't so lucky. Even weirder, some species that had seemed immune at first, like squirrels and deer, became infected later on. In truth, I'd never understood why the disease didn't impact squirrels right away. After all, squirrels are just rats with bushy tails. All I know is that if the disease ever does begin to infect birds, humanity is fucked.

But we're probably fucked anyway.

Once the disease began jumping from species to species, it became unstoppable. America, South America and Canada fell first, followed by Europe, Asia, Africa and then Australia. After that, we lost what little satellite television coverage remained. The last thing any of us saw, as far as I know, was footage of zombies shuffling through the streets of Mumbai.

Of course, the zombies weren't the only threat. There were roving gangs of looters, criminals, extremists and military and law enforcement personnel who'd decided to watch out for themselves, rather than the rest of us. The new law was the law of the gun. Bad enough you had to worry about getting eaten by a dead friend or family member—you also had to worry about getting robbed or raped or murdered by some crazy, antisocial fuckwit taking advantage of the chaos and thriving in the new world disorder.

Not that the powers-that-be had to worry about any of that. Washington D.C. was evacuated early on. They sent President Tyler, the Vice-President, the Cabinet, the Pentagon big-wigs, and all of the House and Senate members and their staff and family to secure underground bunkers in Pennsylvania, Virginia, Maryland and Colorado. Bunkers just like this one, except more modern. I have to wonder if they're in any better shape than we are. Probably. I doubt our leaders are sitting around watching *Aqua Teen Hunger Force* and voting on whether or not to resort to cannibalism. At least, not yet.

I'm so fucking hungry.

This bunker was built as a relocation center back in the early Sixties, when the Cold War was really heating up. President Eisenhower commissioned it, which is why a bronze bust of his head and all the photographs and pictures of him are down here with us. In the event of a nuclear attack on the United States, the bunker was supposed to house the members of the House and the Senate, along with their family members and a few staffers. It was big enough to hold just over a thousand people. To build it, they tunneled eight hundred feet into the side of the mountain, and dug eighty feet underground, as well. No, it wouldn't survive a direct strike from a nuclear warhead, but it was deep enough and secure enough to protect its inhabitants from nuclear firestorms and radioactive fallout. The site was easily accessible from Washington D.C.—it was less than an hour away by railroad or plane, and the interstate ran nearby, as well. Back when the government kept it stocked with supplies, people could have stayed here for up to one-hundred and twenty days.

To prevent the local hillbillies from becoming suspicious during construction, a cover story was devised for the operation. The public was told that a new luxury hotel was being built on top of the mountain, and that it would bring jobs and economic development to the area. And that's exactly what happened. A beautiful, ritzy resort hotel—the Pocahontas (named that because of its location in Pocahontas County)—was erected, and it attracted the wealthy, powerful and elite from around the world. The beautiful people came to visit in droves. Generations of actors, politicians, oil barons, banking magnates and others were among the frequent guests. The hotel employed locals, providing a nice alternative for those who didn't want to slave away in a coal mine, cut timber, try their hand at farming, bend a wrench, or just sit back and collect welfare (these are the five biggest occupations in West Virginia). Over the years, the town grew and expanded. So did The Pocahontas, adding new wings, a golf course, tennis and racquetball courts, stables and an equestrian trail, and even its own private runway for small planes. And in all that time, no one above ground, other than the hotel's administrators, ever suspected what lay beneath the mountain—until one Sunday morning a little over a decade ago, when an investigative reporter for the *New York Times* broke the story on the front page. When that happened, the facility was rendered useless. The government immediately decommissioned the bunker and turned ownership of it over to the hotel. At one point, a data storage company wanted to lease it from the Pocahontas, but the hotel's management had other ideas. They turned it into a museum. For the last ten years, the bunker has been open to visitors and guests of the Pocahontas—an added tourist attraction to an already luxuriant establishment. I should know. I've been one of the bunker's tour guides for the last three years. It was either that, or get a job at Wal Mart, and I fucking hate Wal Mart. And not just because my ex-wife worked there.

That was how I ended up down here with the others. By that point, the shit had already hit the fan in New York and Philly and elsewhere, but it hadn't become widespread. At least, not here. We'd had reports of a few zombies, but West Virginia is such a rural state, with so much wilderness in between our towns, that it didn't seem like an epidemic. It was like watching 9/11 or Hurricane Katrina or one of those other disasters—you knew it was happening and you felt connected to it, but at the same time, it seemed so far away. Bad things always happen to other people. Not to you. Not until the bad things show up at your front door unannounced and come inside and stay for a while.

Martial law hadn't been declared in West Virginia yet, and the hotel was still making us show up for work, even though lodging reservations had dropped to zero. I was standing out back, sneaking a smoke with a few of the Mexican guys from the kitchen, when the dead arrived at the Pocahontas. We smelled them before we saw them, but we didn't know what the stench was or where it was coming from. It was hot outside, and there was only a slight breeze—strong enough only to move the air around rather than cool us off. We all caught a whiff at the same time. I frowned. It was like smelling the world's biggest pile of road kill. That's what I thought it was, at first. I remember wondering if there was a dead groundhog or something somewhere nearby. One of the other guys said something in Spanish. I don't know what it was, because I never learned the language. He probably said something like, "Goddamn, that stinks." Within another minute, the stench grew overpowering. We all looked at each other, frowning and making faces. The Mexican guys talked to each other. I nodded as if I understood them. And then... there they were—shuffling out of the woods and across the parking lot towards us.

Zombies.

I think their silence was the scariest part. The dead were

quiet. No moans or gurgles or cries or shouts. That's not the norm, or at least it didn't remain the norm. Zombies make noise, as a rule. But this group was quiet. It was obvious that they meant business. They bore down on the hotel with an emotionless, single-minded determination, hobbling and pulling themselves forward despite the fact that some of them were missing limbs and major organs, or trailing intestines behind them like leashes. Most of the zombies were human, but there were dead animals, too. Rats, mostly, along with a few foxes and skunks and a black bear cub that was missing an eye and most of its lower jaw. That didn't stop it from coming, though. The dead are determined sons of bitches. Their silence made that determination all the more unnerving.

Two of our groundskeepers drove toward them in a golf cart. To this day, I don't know what those guys were thinking. It's not like they were armed or anything. They were landscapers, not soldiers. I have no idea what they intended to do. Maybe run over the zombies? Whatever their plan was, they never got a chance to see it through. The dead might have been slow, but they could swarm you until there was nowhere left to run. That's what happened with the groundskeepers. They ran over a zombie fox with the golf cart, but the corpse got caught beneath their back wheel and slowed them down. The golf cart shook. Bits of matted fur and decayed flesh were smeared across the pavement. Then, the driver made a sharp turn. I guess he was trying to dislodge the dead critter. Problem was, golf carts aren't made for hairpin turns. He tipped the fucking thing over on its side, and before either man could scramble free of the wreckage, the zombies were on them from all sides—penning them in. One man started screaming as the dead shuffled closer. The other one sank to his knees and began praying in Spanish and frantically crossing himself. It was a slow death for them both. The zombies crowded in, closer and closer, until both the golf cart and the victims were lost from sight. Their screams became whimpers, and then turned into screams again. One zombie thrust its arm in the air, as if in triumph, clutching a hunk of raw, red, dripping meat.

That was all the rest of us needed to see. We turned and

fled, shoving and tripping each other in our hurry to get away. Behind us came the most awful sounds—tearing and ripping and biting. By then, the screams had ceased. We ran back into the hotel, only to learn that the shit had hit the fan inside the Pocahontas, as well. Zombies surged in through both the main entrance and the doors to the meditation garden. They swarmed through the lobby and around the elevators and were beginning to make their way down the long concourse of ritzy stores and shops that occupy most of the hotel's first floor—jewelers, a humidor, candy stores, coffee shops, a bookstore, clothing stores and other businesses catering to the guests because none of the locals in town could ever afford to shop in them.

I ran into my buddy Mike, who worked in the hotel's banqueting department. Looking back on it now, it's all Mike's fault that I'm in this goddamned situation. He reached out and grabbed my shoulders, stopping me in mid-run. At first, I was so scared that I didn't even recognize him. I tried pushing him away, but he squeezed harder. My hands curled into fists.

"Let go of me, asshole! Don't you see what's happening?"

"The bunker," he yelled. "We've got to get everyone into the bunker, Pete."

And just like that, everything changed. It was like Mike had uttered some magic words. I was still scared, but my head was clearer. I started thinking about survival, rather than just running around in blind panic. My fear wasn't ruling me. I was ruling it. It felt very Zen. People ran by us, tripping and stumbling and crying. The hallway was filled with screams and shouts. All of these things seemed distant. Remote. Disconnected from us. I suddenly felt like an island.

"The bunker…hell, why didn't I think of that?"

"You've got a key, right?"

I nodded. As one of the tour guides, I had one of seven plastic key cards that would let us into the bunker. I was about to speak, when I noticed Mike's eyes grow wide. He bit his lip but I don't think he was aware that he was doing it. He stared at something over my shoulder. I turned around, wincing at the sudden stench. A group of zombies were shambling toward us.

"Shit."

"Tell everyone you can," Mike said. "I'll meet you down there."

"Where are you going?"

"The kitchen. There's no telling how long we'll be down there. We'll need food and water."

"Good idea. I'll come with you."

"No, Pete. You need to let everyone else know. I'll take care of getting the supplies."

"You can't carry all that stuff by yourself."

"I'll load it up on a cart and use the service elevator. That opens up right into the conference center. Long as you've got the bunker door open, it'll be fine."

I frowned. "Are you sure?"

He nodded. "Positive. Now go."

"Be careful."

"You, too. Just make sure you keep that door open for me."

I promised him that I would, and then he ran down the hall, easily dodging the dead. His movements reminded me of a football player charging toward the end zone, intent on a touchdown. By the time the zombies reached for him, he was already past them. I turned the other way and headed for the bunker.

The next time I saw Mike, his throat had been torn out, his nose was hanging by a flap of skin, and one of his eyes was missing. That didn't stop him, though. He showed up at the bunker door, just like he'd said he would.

And then he tried to eat me.

***

There were two entrances to the bunker. The first one was via an outdoor tunnel on the other side of the mountain, some distance from the hotel. Normally, when we gave visitors a tour, we started from that entrance after taking them there via a short bus ride. The entrance had a ten foot high steel blast door with a big sign affixed to it that said DANGER: HIGH VOLTAGE. The sign had originally been put there to scare people away—random hikers or hunters who might have stumbled across it—but it was obsolete now. The Pocahontas kept the sign there as part of the ambience. Since the bunker was now nothing more than a museum, it added a touch of authenticity.

The other entrance was located inside the hotel itself, adjacent to our basement-level conference center. The conference center was a huge, open room where various organizations and groups held conventions, employee meetings, dinners, and things like that. It was a very plain room. The carpet was thin and worn. The overhead lights were too bright. The walls were a drab off-white color. I once overheard a hotel guest refer to the décor as "wholly uninspiring." But one of those uninspiring walls concealed the bunker's second entrance. When the partition was slid back, it revealed a second steel blast door, bigger than the door guarding the outside tunnel entrance. It was twelve feet high and twelve feet wide and weighed over twenty-five tons. Despite its size, the blast door was easy to open from the inside. Any healthy person could have done it. There was a wheel you turned to open or close the door, and all you had to do was apply fifty pounds of pressure. On tours, we always exited the bunker through this door, and it always took our guests by surprise when they emerged back into the hotel.

A shriek brought me back to my surroundings. A woman's voice. I couldn't tell whose, shouting about something biting her face.

The zombies flooded into the lobby and there was no time to wait for an elevator. I took the stairs two at a time and paused at the bottom of the stairwell. I put my ear to the door and listened, trying to determine if the conference center was safe or not, but I couldn't tell. The screams from upstairs were too loud. Taking a deep breath, I slowly nudged the door open and peeked into the room. Either Mike's warning had been heard, or others had the same idea as him, because there were a group of about twenty-five people cowering by the wall. About half of the group were folks I knew—employees of the hotel. The other half of the group looked like hotel guests or visitors. One big guy had a cable repairman's uniform on.

My friend Drew was among them, and I felt better when I saw him. I stepped through the door and hurried over to them.

"Pete!" Drew rushed toward me. "Tell me you've got a key to get inside?"

Nodding, I pulled the keycard from my back pocket. Drew sighed with obvious relief.

"Thank Christ. I thought we were gonna be trapped down here."

The group milled around me, blocking my access to the partition. Behind us, something thudded in the stairwell. They scrambled out of the way, and I hurried over to the wall and pushed the partition into its recess, revealing the blast door. The sounds in the stairwell grew louder. I flashed my keycard. The lock disengaged, and I turned the wheel. The door rumbled open with a deep, ominous boom.

"Everybody inside!"

I didn't need to tell them twice. The group hurried into the bunker, jostling one another in the process. Drew was at the rear of the procession. He paused when he realized that I wasn't following.

"Aren't you coming?"

I shook my head. "I've got to wait for Mike. He went back to the kitchen to get us some supplies."

Drew glanced at the stairwell and elevator doors and then back at me. His eyes were wide and his expression grim. "Do you think he can make it?"

"He's got to. Otherwise, we'll starve. There's no food in there. Just a vending machine with sodas and chips and shit."

From behind us, someone asked, "What's the hold up?"

Drew and I turned. It was the cable repairman. He stared at us in confusion. Fear had made his face taught and pale. He had a receding hairline and his forehead was slick with sweat. He smelled sour. This close, I could read the name sewn above the pocket of his uniform: CHUCK.

"We're waiting on somebody," I said.

Chuck blinked. "But those things…"

"Aren't down here yet. My friend Mike went to get food and supplies. Soon as he gets here, we'll close the door."

"Screw that," someone else called. I couldn't tell who it was. The group was standing all bunched together like sardines in a can. "If you want to hang around and wait for your friend, go ahead. But close the damned door first."

"I'll be honest, Pete," Drew said. "I tend to agree with them."

"We're okay down here," I insisted. "The zombies are on the lobby level."

Then the stairwell door banged open and a corpse tumbled into the conference room, making a liar out of me. I glanced over at the service elevator. The doors remained shut and the light above them indicated that the elevator was still on the lobby level. I gritted my teeth, fighting the urge to run inside the bunker and seal the door.

"Damn it, Mike…"

The first zombie tottered to its feet and stared at us. Then it lurched forward, grasping with one hand. Its other arm hung limp at its side, obviously broken in several places. Shards of splintered bone stuck out of the torn flesh like porcupine quills. Its mouth hung open, and its grayish-white tongue dangled like a slug. It took another step. Two more corpses emerged from the stairwell and followed along behind it. Then another.

"Come on, Pete." Drew tugged at my shoulder. "We've got to go."

"We have to wait for Mike."

"He's obviously not coming," another man said. I found out later that his name was Jim Mars. "We wait any longer, and we're dead."

"He's right, Pete," Drew said. "Come on!"

I shrugged free of Drew's grip and glanced at the elevator again. The light had gone on, indicating that it was moving.

"We go in there without food," I said, "and we're dead anyway."

"We'll make due. We only have to wait a few days. Sooner or later, when we don't come out, they'll get bored and wander away."

The zombies crept closer. Behind us, the group in the bunker echoed Drew's sentiments, urging me to close the door. Then Chuck stepped forward.

21

"Look," he said, "fuck this. If you don't want to come, then that's your own business. Stay here and get eaten. But we're closing the door."

I started to get in his face, but then the elevator dinged and the doors opened. We all turned to look. Mike stepped out of the elevator. Even if he hadn't been so obviously mangled, I'd have known something was wrong with him right away because his movements were jerky and halting. I cringed, unable to turn away from the damage he'd suffered in the short time since I'd last seen him. In addition to his missing eye and throat, and his nearly-severed nose (which dangled by one flap of skin and banged against his cheek each time he took a step), the crotch of Mike's pants were a bloody mess. I wasn't sure, but it looked like his dick had been ripped off.

He wasn't alone in the elevator. There was a wheeled cart inside, just beyond the open doors, loaded down with canned goods and boxes of dry food and cases of bottled spring water. A first aid kit sat atop the supplies. There were also five more zombies milling about the cart. They trailed after Mike, staring at us with blank expressions. Their mouths were crimson and shiny. The lights in the conference center flickered and dimmed, then grew bright again. It made the blood on their faces seem that much more garish.

With the dead converging on us now from two different directions, there was no way to get to the cart. Even as I considered it, the elevator doors slid shut. The zombies didn't notice. They were focused solely on us. I glanced around for a weapon, but there was nothing. Sighing, I turned to Chuck.

"Come on then. Get inside."

He did. Drew followed along behind him, leaving me standing alone. Mike's shoes squeaked on the tiled floor as he closed the distance between us. I stared into his eyes, wondering if there was any shred of consciousness left.

"Mike?" My voice cracked. My throat felt dry and swollen. "You still in there, dude?"

He reached for my hand, and his teeth snapped together. Flinching, I turned and ran inside the bunker. Behind me, Mike moaned. It was a hungry, mournful sound.

"Hurry up," Chuck shouted. "They're going to get in!"

I slid the blast door shut behind us. It rumbled, slipping into place and then clicked as it locked. A hissing sound faded as the door sealed.

"Will it hold?" A woman pushed forward through the crowd. "Can they get inside here?"

I shook my head, and explained the blast door to them, realizing as I did it that I had slipped into my tour guide speech. When I was finished, I asked them if they had any questions. Turned out that they did. Lots of questions. I spent the next twenty minutes answering them. I gave them the whole spiel, including an abbreviated version of the bunker's history and how it benefited us in our current situation. When I was done, we stood there for a while. Nobody spoke. The sound of our breathing echoed softly in the hall. Beneath it was an even quieter sound, barely noticeable unless you concentrated on it—a steady, monotonous drumbeat.

"What is that?" Drew whispered.

"The dead," I said, "pounding on the door."

Chuck frowned. "And you're sure they can't get in?"

"I'm positive. They can't get in, but as long as they stay on the other side of the door, we can't get out this way, either. We'll have to use the other entrance."

"What if there are zombies around it, too?" Drew ran a hand through his hair. His eyes were wide and wet.

I shrugged. "Then we might be here for a while."

Turned out I was right. There were more zombies around the other entrance, and that was how we ended up trapped inside the bunker. It takes forty to fifty days for the average human being to die of starvation, provided they have water to drink. We've been here for a little over a month now. What little food we had—stuff from the vending machine and breath mints a few survivors had in their purses—ran out in the first week. Even if we'd done a better job of rationing it, those supplies wouldn't have lasted. We've got plenty of water. I'm not thirsty, but I'm fucking starving. I'm as hungry as the persistent dead still lingering around outside the doors.

TWO

I was still sitting in the movie room when Drew rushed in. Much like the day when we'd first entered the bunker, his eyes were wide and his expression was panicked. He was breathing hard, and when I asked him what was wrong, he held up a finger, indicating that I should wait. He bent over, put his hands on his knees, and gulped air. He sounded like he was dying. His face was red from exertion and sweat lathered his forehead and cheeks. I waited for him to catch his breath.

"What's wrong?" I placed a hand on his shoulder. He was warm, and his shirt was damp with perspiration. "Are you having a heart attack or something?"

He shook his head and gasped. "They just voted…Chuck and the rest."

"So it's finished, then? Well, thank God that's over with. Now we can get back to figuring out an alternative. Come up with a real plan."

"No…they voted…to do it. They voted yes."

I didn't say anything. I couldn't. I was too stunned. I'd been scoffing at this insanity ever since Chuck had first proposed it. I hadn't taken it seriously, and I'd figured most of the others wouldn't either. Well, none of the sane people in our group, at least. A few might consider it—those who were cracking from the strain of our situation. But I'd always assumed that in the end, clearer heads would prevail. I'd been positive that the majority of us wouldn't vote for something as totally fucked up as cannibalism via lottery. That's why I hadn't even attended the group meeting with everyone else. I'd figured the others would tell Chuck they were voting 'No' and that would put an end to the whole crazy idea. After all, who in their right mind would actually vote for allowing themselves a one in twenty-six chance of ending up as dinner for the rest of us?

24

Apparently, quite a few.

"They voted in favor of it?" My voice was barely a whisper. "In *favor?*"

Drew nodded. "Yeah. It was unanimous—except for me. I voted against it, of course."

"Nobody else? Not even the Chinese guy?"

"He voted in favor, too."

"But he doesn't even speak English. How did he know what they were voting on?"

Drew shrugged.

"So, you and I are the only sane motherfuckers left down here?"

"It sure seems like it. What are we going to do, Pete?"

"I don't know, brother. I don't know."

Eisenhower watched us, his bronze face expressionless. *Aqua Teen Hunger Force* still played on the big screen— Master Shake and Meatwad were singing a song about zombies. The irony made my stomach churn. I idly wished that I'd watched *Reba* instead. If I was going to die, it would have been better to go out jerking off to Joanna Garcia rather than watching a bunch of cartoon characters, no matter how funny they were.

Drew stood up. I was happy to see that both his complexion and his breathing were slowly returning to normal. It would have been a hell of a thing if he'd died of a heart attack before our fellow survivors had a chance to kill and eat him properly. He glanced out into the hallway and then quietly shut the door

"Jesus…" I shook my head in disbelief. "I can't believe this shit."

"There's more, Pete. It gets worse."

"How can it get any worse?"

"Since you didn't attend the meeting, Chuck and the others decided…shit, I don't know how to say this."

"Decided what? Just tell me what the hell is going on."

"They decided…they decided that you should be first. They…they said that was only fair, since everybody else was willing to vote even though it might be them that got picked. Chuck said that since you didn't have the balls to show up, you were being disrespectful to the rest of them. They all agreed. Well, maybe agreed isn't the right word, but they all went along with it. So, instead of a lottery to decide who feeds the rest of us, they've picked you to be the first."

"Fuck you."

"I'm not kidding. You've got to get the hell out of here, Pete. They're coming."

I stood there, stunned. My arms hung limp and numb at my sides. My hands and fingers tingled as if asleep. My asshole puckered and my balls shrank. There was a feeling in my stomach, a sensation I'd only felt once before in my life on the day my wife of eight years, Alyssa, told me she was leaving me and that she wanted a divorce. I sat on the couch that day, wanting desperately to flee, to run away from her, to get out of the range of the things she was saying, because if I couldn't hear her say them, then they wouldn't come true—but I was unable to move. On that day, my body felt like it temporarily belonged to someone else. Now I had that feeling once again, to paraphrase that old Pink Floyd song, except that in real life, my numbness was anything but comfortable. Instead, it was like drowning in a bathtub full of ice. Drew said something to me, but I couldn't understand him. The ringing in my ears was too loud. I watched his lips, trying to read them. He grabbed my shoulders and shook me hard.

"Come on," he urged again. "You've got to go, Pete. Snap out of it. You've got to run, right fucking now."

"Where are they?" It was hard to form the words. My tongue felt thick.

"Last I saw, they were all still in the dining room."

"Well, that's appropriate."

"They were debating how to proceed. Some of them said we should tell it to you straight—we owed you that, as decent human beings."

I choked down laughter and bile. Drew didn't notice.

"A couple people said we should just wait until you went to sleep, and capture you then, but Chuck and the others said that we should act before that. Then they started debating how. By that point, I was already slipping out the door to come warn you. As far as I know, they're still debating, but it won't be much longer. They'll come for you. That's why you've got to go now, man."

"But where? The reason they're having this vote is because we're trapped in here. Where the hell am I supposed to go, Drew?"

"I don't know."

I shook my head in despair. "I can't go outside or into the hotel. The zombies are still there, hanging around both sets of blast doors. I mean, what kind of choice is that? Leave the bunker and get eaten by the dead, or stay here and get eaten by the living? Either way, I'm screwed."

"Just hide, then."

"Hide? Hide *where*, exactly? We're in a bunker, Drew. And what the hell am I supposed to do when they find me? And they *will* find me. What then? Talk my way out of it? We don't have any weapons down here. Sure, we've got kitchen utensils and tools and shit, but I can't fight my way out of here with a fucking butter knife."

Drew paused for a moment. Then, with an excited grin, he snapped his fingers and grabbed my arm.

"What about the power plant? It's dark and crowded and there's all kinds of places to hide in between the transformers and the generators and stuff. Best of all, it's so loud in there. They'll never hear you over those generators. Hide there. I can bring you water, whenever I get a chance."

"Until they catch you," I said. "Then we'll both be dinner."

"Well, I don't know what other options you—"

He stopped suddenly as the sound of footsteps echoed down the hall, coming toward us. The fear returned to Drew's eyes. He glanced around the room frantically.

"Quick—*hide!*"

I had two choices—stand behind the door or duck down behind Eisenhower's display. If I hid behind the door, there was a chance that whoever opened it would see me. It was dark in the room, except for the glow from the television, but if they pushed the door too far and it struck me, I'd be discovered. I glanced at the small stand that Eisenhower's bust sat on. If whoever was coming stood at certain spots in the room, they'd surely see me crouched down behind it. My only hope was that the room's dim lighting might work to my advantage.

Muffled voices echoed in the corridor, unintelligible beneath the DVD soundtrack. The footsteps stopped in front of the door. Drew and I stared at each other. One set of footsteps walked away. I took a deep breath and held it. Then the doorknob started to turn. Exhaling, I leaped over the chairs and dove behind the Eisenhower bust display just as the door started to open.

"Where is he, Drew?"

I recognized the speaker from his voice. It was Krantz, one of Chuck's cronies. I'm not sure what he'd done before the zombies took over. I don't think he ever mentioned it. Whatever his previous vocation, down here in the bunker, he'd been a toadie and a boot-licker—one of those guys who attach themselves to the alpha male of the pack and do whatever they ask in an effort to be accepted, liked and protected. He was in his mid-forties, balding, and cursed with the worst case of Rosacea I'd ever seen. He had chronically bloodshot, runny eyes and his face was a network of spider-web veins. His nose looked like a rotten fruit. When we'd first entered the bunker, he'd also had a prodigious gut. Now, like the rest of us, he'd undergone drastic weight loss. The lack of food had just made his skin condition that much worse.

"Hey, Krantz. I was just coming to find you guys."

Drew sounded nervous. I held my breath, wondering if Krantz would notice. He did.

"Don't bullshit me, Drew. I'm not in the mood. Where's your buddy?"

"Pete?"

"No, the fucking Tooth Fairy."

"I don't know where he is."

"Don't fuck with me, Drew. I mean it. This can go one of two ways for you, and I don't think you'll like the second option."

"I'm telling you, I don't know where he is. Seriously. I came to look for him. Figure he'd be in here, since he spends a lot of time watching movies. But he wasn't. I was just about to head back and tell you guys. Is the meeting over?"

Instead of responding, Krantz began to search the room. I heard his footsteps, slow and deliberate. Drew coughed. On the screen, the credits rolled.

"He's not in here. Maybe he's asleep."

"So who was watching this cartoon, then? I doubt that it turned itself on."

"I guess he must have been in here before."

"And where is he now?"

"I told you, I don't know."

"You're lying, Drew."

I peeked out from behind my hiding place. Krantz was standing directly in front of me, but he had his back turned. His hands were on his hips. Drew was facing him. Drew's expression had gone slack.

"Come on," Krantz said. "Let's go."

"Go where?"

"You can explain this to Chuck."

"Explain what?"

"Why you're lying. Why you're hiding Pete. Maybe we'll just go with you instead. Might make things easier all around."

Drew shook his head. "I'm telling you, I don't know where Pete is. I'm not lying. I just—"

He moved fast, surprising both Krantz and myself. One moment he was talking, and the next, he'd thrown a punch at Krantz's throat, connecting with the man's Adam's apple. Krantz stumbled backward, grasping at his neck, and toppled to the floor. He made choking sounds, and when he saw me, his eyes went wide, bulging in their sockets. He thrashed on the floor, writhing, trying to breathe and failing miserably. He reached for me with one hand.

Without thinking about it, I pushed Eisenhower's bronze bust off of its pedestal, dropping it directly onto Krantz's head. The sound was like an overripe watermelon bursting. Blood splattered all over me, and then I couldn't see Krantz's eyes anymore. His arms and legs jittered, and a dark, wet stain appeared on the crotch of his pants. Then he lay still.

"Holy shit…" Drew gaped.

I stood up. The room smelled like piss. My vision was blurry. I wiped my eyes with my hands, smearing Krantz's blood. I took a step toward Drew and my foot slipped in the gore.

"Holy shit," Drew said again. "I guess he doesn't have to worry about his Rosacea anymore."

He giggled, but it was a strange, bleak sound. There was no humor in Drew's voice, and his expression was grim. I knew how he felt. I tried to swallow, and found that I couldn't. My stomach fluttered.

"Tell them I did this," I said.

"But then they'll—"

"Tell them" I interrupted. "Otherwise, they'll be after you, too. Tell them you and he came in here, and I surprised you both."

"But—"

"We don't have time to argue, Drew. I've got to go."

I stuck my head into the hall. The coast was clear. There was no sign of whoever else Krantz had been talking to. Maybe they were searching another room. Whatever the case, I made a break for it, praying they wouldn't step back into the hall at that moment. I glanced back only once, and saw Drew staring after me, clearly still in shock. He lifted one hand and waved at me.

Then I ran.

***

I guess it would help if I described the bunker's layout. It feels like a labyrinth until you learn your way around, but once you get used to it, the layout is pretty straightforward. The bunker covers just over one-hundred and thirteen thousand square feet. If you entered it from the hotel (which was currently occupied by hordes of zombies), after the blast door, you'd walk down a short corridor which opened into the dining room. This is a large area. It had to be, when you consider how many people would have eaten there in the event of a nuclear war. Beyond the dining room was the infirmary, pharmacy, dorm rooms and several lounges, as well as the library and the media room. Most of these had been converted into exhibits for the tours.

They still had some of the original equipment and supplies that the government had kept here when the bunker was still active. Sadly, none of these supplies included food.

As I ran, I thought about hiding in one of the dorm rooms or the infirmary, but quickly decided against it. Given their close proximity to the dining room, that was where most of the others would be. My only choice was to go in the other direction, deeper into the mountain. The corridor I fled down was the same as all of the other hallways in the facility—garish white linoleum floors and drab, featureless concrete walls. The monotony was broken only by the occasional exhibit or 'Exit' sign. Those exit signs were the biggest joke of all. The irony hadn't been lost on any of us. There was no exit from the bunker, except in death.

I raced by the restrooms and then through a set of double doors, which led into another corridor. On my left was the incinerator room. It was diesel-powered and burned hot enough to incinerate human bones. The government had intended it to be that way, in case survivors in the bunker had to dispose of their dead, or rid the facility of radioactive or contaminated clothing. Before the arrival of the zombies, the hotel had used the incinerator to burn up trash, so it was well-stocked with diesel fuel. Since first coming down here, we'd run it a few times to keep warm, but it had mostly sat empty.

I paused in front of the incinerator room and listened. The hallway was quiet. I turned around and peeked through the double doors. The corridor was still empty. If the others had discovered Krantz's death, then they hadn't organized yet. Even still, the hunt was on now. They'd be coming for me soon. My heart pounded, pulsing in my throat. Common sense dictated that I should keep running, but I was scared and tired and panicked, and I decided instead to hide inside the incinerator room. I went inside and closed the door behind me, debating whether or not to turn on the lights. With the door shut, it was so dark inside that I couldn't see anything, and after stumbling around for a few seconds, I fumbled for the light switch. It felt sticky and cold beneath my fingers. I clicked it on and the fluorescents buzzed to life overhead, flooding the room with their harsh brilliance.

I glanced around, looking for a weapon or a place to hide. The incinerator room was a large, gray-cinderblock area. Despite its size, there wasn't much room inside because the incinerator itself dominated the space. It was a big, metal beast with a large, hinged iron door. A ventilation shaft ran from the top of the unit up into the ceiling. A second shaft ran from the ceiling down into the incinerator. This second shaft was a burn chute that went to the bunker's decontamination center, one floor above. In the event of a nuclear war, survivors could have shed their irradiated clothing, which could then be sent down the chute and burned. The other ventilation shaft acted as a chimney. It exited somewhere atop the mountain, far away from the hotel. I knew there was no way I could escape through it, though. We'd tried that early on in the siege, only to learn that the ductwork narrowed steadily the further it went. A human being wouldn't have been able to fit through it. I glanced down at my skinny frame, wondering if maybe I could chance it now. Then I shuddered at the thought of getting stuck. Facing down the mob in the bunker was better than slowly starving to death while trapped in a tube.

Of course, I was starving to death down here, too.

Still, either option was preferable to facing down the dead, and even if I did make it out of the tube, I'd still have the zombies to contend with. I knew they were still sequestered around the blast doors, even without opening the doors to check. We'd been able to hear them milling around out there. The dead aren't quiet. They're anything but. They moan and growl and bump into things. They'd remained at the blast doors. Could they be gathered around the chimney pipe, as well? I didn't know—and decided the possibility of getting stuck in the tube wasn't worth the risk of finding out.

You might be asking yourself why the dead hung around for so long? If they couldn't get inside the bunker to eat us, why didn't they just move on in search of easier prey? Well, it's because they're stupid. Their bodies may be reanimated, but their brains certainly aren't—at least, the part of their brain that solves problems and figures things out via logic and

32

thought. Sure, they have their basic motor skills. They can walk and grasp and bite like a motherfucker, but they have no deductive reasoning. They saw us go inside the bunker, so they milled around the blast doors, waiting for us to come out. More zombies arrived and joined the others. Sooner or later, the first group of zombies probably forgot that we were in here, but by then, there are so many of them crowded around the doors, they mimic each other. If one zombie sees another banging on the door, it does the same. And they stay there until they rot away, or something else distracts them.

In the first few days of the siege, we tried to do that very thing—distract the zombies that were waiting on the other side of the blast door inside the hotel. We sent two volunteers, Rachel and Milo, to the bunker's other exit. Rachel ran for her high school's cross country team and Milo was a personal trainer who worked in the hotel's gym. Both of them could run, and were in good shape. The plan seemed so simple. They'd sneak out of the bunker via the other blast door, make their way down the mountainside and through the woods, and then let the zombies inside the hotel see them. When those zombies began to follow them away from the blast doors, Rachel and Milo would run back to the other exit and get inside before the zombies could catch them. Then the zombies would lose interest and leave. Except things didn't quite turn out that way. There were more zombies in the woods than we had originally planned on. Rachel and Milo hadn't made it twenty-five yards past the exit when a corpse shambled out from behind a tree and made a grab for Milo. The personal trainer—this athletic, Adonis-like man—dodged the zombie, tripped over a root, and fell down, banging up his knee and twisting his ankle in the process. The creature had its rotten teeth in Milo's throat before Rachel could even react. She panicked, and instead of helping Milo (although at that point, the only way to have aided him would have been to bash his brains out) she started running back toward the blast door. We hollered, cheering her on and urging her not to look back. For a brief moment, we thought for sure she'd make it back inside without being noticed, as Milo's killer was busy gorging itself on his flesh. But two more zombies emerged from the woods and saw her. Rachel made it back inside, but by then it was too late. They knew we were in here. Then we had zombies at both exits.

They've been there ever since.

Rachel killed herself a few days later. She swallowed an entire bottle of Advil that she'd had in her purse. It wasn't a quick death, nor was it painless. When we put her in the incinerator, her abdomen was swollen and hard. I can't imagine what that many painkillers did to her liver. She popped when she burned.

My thoughts turned back to the business at hand. Musing over Milo and Rachel would only insure that I ended up dead like them, and I was determined not to let that happen. I needed something—anything—to defend myself with. There weren't a lot of items or tools inside the incinerator room, and as a result, my choice of weapons was less than inspiring. A red fire extinguisher, covered in a thick layer of ash and dust, hung on the wall. It would be heavy and unwieldy. A long iron bar with a blunt hook on one end was leaning against the wall next to it. We used the bar to shove things into the incinerator and stir the ashes around, but it wouldn't be of much use in defending myself with. It was heavy, and its length and the limited amount of space in the room meant I would have trouble swinging it around or thrusting. I decided instead to use the rod to bar the door. I slid it through the door handle. Both ends of the iron bar lined up flat against the wall. Satisfied that this would prevent anyone from pulling the door open, I slumped down to the floor with my back against the cold incinerator, and took an opportunity to catch my breath.

I hadn't realized until that moment that I was trembling. My skin was covered with goose bumps and the hair on my arms stood up as if I'd been shocked with static electricity. I suddenly felt very cold. At first, I thought it must be the chilly metal surface of the incinerator, but when I slid forward and moved away from it, the feeling didn't subside. Instead, it grew worse. My teeth started to chatter and the shaking intensified. I belched, wincing at the smell. My mouth tasted sour. I burped again, shivering all over now. My stomach cramped and then I felt pressure building in my throat. I leaned over, involuntarily brought my hand up to my mouth, and then vomited through my fingers. Even my puke felt cold. It ran down my wrist and arm and splattered all over my lap, soaking my clothes. The stench was terrible. There were no solids in it, seeing as how I hadn't eaten anything in…well, since we'd run out of food. It was all liquid, and I cringed when I noticed a brownish-red tint to it. That couldn't be good.

My stomach cramped again, forcing me to bend over far enough that the tip of my nose touched the cold concrete floor. The dry heaves came next, followed by more burps. I guess my body wasn't satisfied with that, because then the gas started coming out the other end. At that point, I was beyond caring. I lay there shaking and moaning in my own filth and stink, and waited for the tempest to subside. I thought about what I'd just done—killing Krantz. The magnitude of my actions was unshakeable. I thought about the sound his head had made when I squashed it with Eisenhower's bronze bust. I wondered if I'd ever be able to forget that sound.

I wrapped my arms around myself and lay down on the floor, curling into the fetal position. I was soaked with my own puke and cold and hungry and miserable, and I felt like crying, but that would have been a waste of valuable fluids. The remorse weighed heavily on me. I told myself that Krantz had left me no choice. No choice at all. If I hadn't killed him, then Drew and I would be dead by now. Certainly I would be, at least, and that was reason enough to do what I'd done. It was pure survival. Nothing else. You do what you have to do to stay alive.

I repeated this to myself over and over again, but it didn't really help. I'd done a lot of bad things in my life, but they all paled in comparison to committing murder. I'd just killed someone. Not someone who was already dead, but a living, breathing human being. That topped the bill of the list of things I'd done wrong in my life.

Thinking about those wrongs made me think about Alyssa, my ex-wife, which brought new pangs to my stomach—not of hunger and revulsion, but of guilt and regret. I lay there, wishing I could die and hating myself for fighting it when I'd had the opportunity to do so just moments before.

THREE

When I was five years old, my parents took my little sister and me on vacation to Virginia Beach. The hotel had a nice, outdoor swimming pool, and on our way from the hotel room down to the beach, as we were walking by the pool, I reached out and pushed my little sister in. It wasn't a malicious act. There was no forethought. No planning. I don't know why I did it then and I still don't know today. She was just a toddler. She could barely walk, let alone swim. My father jumped in and pulled her out before the hotel's lifeguard could even react. My sister was okay. She cried and sputtered and coughed water. I cried and sputtered and spent the rest of that day grounded in the hotel room, with a sore bottom, unable to watch TV or read comic books or do anything but wither under the angry, reproachful glare of my father. Looking back on it now, I suspect there were other emotions in his eyes other than just anger. I think he was scared—frightened by what his little boy had just done. Him and my mother both were. When her and my sister got back from the beach, they made me apologize. The next day, it was like nothing had ever happened, but I was aware, even at the age of five, that they watched me a little more carefully.

That's the first bad thing I remember doing.

I did other bad things as a kid. I shoplifted a pack of bubble gum cards once. I cheated on a Social Studies test. I boxed Tom Schoen's ears so hard in shop class that he had to miss a few days of school because of persistent ringing in them. I wasn't some juvenile delinquent, nor was I a bully, but I did have a tendency, even back then, to put myself and my own needs first above others. I'd wanted the gum cards but didn't have the money to buy them, so I'd justified my actions by telling myself that it was only once, and I didn't get caught so it was okay. My mantra was always "Do whatever you have to do to survive." That's something that carried over into adulthood, though I never recognized that flaw in myself until after my wife had left me and I started going to counseling.

I met Alyssa when both of us were fresh out of college and working third shift together at the local convenience store. We used to laugh about that. She'd majored in secondary education at West Virginia University and I'd been a business major at North Carolina State—and yet we'd both ended up back here, working the graveyard shift in a convenience store because there weren't any other jobs to be found. After a few weeks of working with her, I didn't care. Alyssa was amazing. She was totally unlike any girl I'd ever met, even the ones from college. She was smart and clever and funny and an absolute knock-out. I'd always done okay when it came to women. I mean, I certainly wasn't a virgin by any means. I'd had my fair share of girlfriends in high school and college. But I'd never been with a girl as beautiful as Alyssa was. And when we started dating, it was wild and weird and scary. I fell for her. Hard.

Alyssa suffered from chronic depression. As a result, she took a lot of antidepressants. I didn't know much about the disease, at least, not then. I was young and stupid and concerned mostly with my own feelings and emotions. I simplified her condition in my mind, chalking her depression up to "She's unhappy. I can make her happy." So I tried. I tried like hell. I did everything I could think of. I bought her flowers not just on Valentine's Day or her birthday, but in the middle of the week, not for any special occasion, but just because I loved her. I left her notes inside books she was reading. I took her on surprise picnics. Showed her things and places from my childhood and involved her in my life. I was nice to her friends and her parents. I called every night, just to tell her that I loved her. I made her laugh. Made her smile. Made her feel safe and wanted and important. And when the depression didn't go away, I told myself it was because I wasn't good enough. I wasn't good enough to make her happy. It was my own insecurities talking, but again, I didn't know that at the time. Another problem was that the anti-depressants impacted our sex life. Alyssa wasn't in the mood very often, and on the rare occasions when she was, the medication prevented her from achieving orgasm. It was frustrating for her, but looking back, I was more concerned for my own feelings. I took it personally. I was the reason she couldn't enjoy sex. It was me, not the meds. I wasn't good enough. She told me again and again that this wasn't so, that it wasn't me, that it was just the antidepressants, but deep down inside, I never believed her.

Still, I figured if I hung in there, things would work out. I loved her, after all. It would get better in time. We moved in together, and began to argue about little things, same as what happens in all relationships at a certain point. We squabbled over money, mostly. I'd begin working at the hotel by then, and Alyssa had gotten an office job. She made more money than I did, and between the two of us, we did alright, but things were still tight. We wanted to save enough to get married, but we never seemed able to do so, because there were always other things I thought we needed—a flat-screen television, a trip to Cancun, a new truck when the transmission burned out in mine. I began hiding little purchases from her. I'd go out to a bar after work and hide the receipt. I'd buy a new video game or DVD and tell her someone gave it to me. Little lies, told with the best of intentions. I wanted to please her more than anything. I wanted her to be happy. I wanted her to stop worrying about finances. But because I was a self-centered prick, I didn't want those concerns to impact my own happiness. I didn't want to go without the things I needed, be they something as trivial as a video game or something as monumental as Alyssa's love. So I lied in order to please her and keep her, and each time she found out about it, Alyssa pulled away a little bit more. The emotional distance between us grew wider. Back then, I told myself it was her depression, but I know now that it was because of me and my actions.

I grew close to Hannah, a girl who worked the hotel's registration desk Monday through Friday. She was just a friend, but Alyssa resented the time I spent with her, and I resented Alyssa's resentment. It wasn't like I was having an affair or anything. All Hannah and I ever did was talk. Eventually, I found myself telling her things and sharing things with her that, for one reason or another, I couldn't share with Alyssa. We began hanging out together, always in a group, with other friends, but sitting aside one another, laughing together, having fun. Alyssa confronted me about it, and I protested once more, assuring her that there was nothing going on. I told her she was being paranoid and jealous, and in my mind, I believed that to be so, because I hadn't realized I was entering into an emotional affair with Hannah. I honestly saw her as just a friend—someone who could be emotionally intimate with me in ways that Alyssa could not. I didn't want to lose Alyssa. I loved her. But she couldn't give me what I needed, so I sought it elsewhere, and where was the harm in that? You do what you have to do to survive.

Despite our problems, Alyssa and I got married and ended up buying a little house. My friendship with Hannah waxed and waned. When Alyssa and I were having problems, Hannah always seemed to be there, ready to step up and open herself to me emotionally. We flirted somewhat, and joked about sex once or twice, but I never slept with her. I never even considered it until eight years later when Alyssa told me that she wanted a divorce. I remember that day so clearly. I'd come home from work, surprised to find Alyssa already home, as well. I gave her the customary hug and a peck on the forehead, but she felt distant and stiff. By then, I was used to that reaction from her, so I simply walked away and sat down on the couch. I had turned on a video game and was just getting ready to play when I realized that she was standing next to me. I noticed then that she'd been crying. Without a word, she sat down next to me and began to talk, and the things she told me about myself and about our marriage were the most awful things I have ever heard, because they were true. They were all true. I'd just never realized them until then. I was a self-centered, immature asshole who had lied to her and treated her like shit and had been engaged in an emotional affair with a co-worker for the entire eight years of our marriage. The worst part, she said, was that she knew I had the best of intentions. She knew

I didn't mean to hurt her. I was just too selfish to realize that my efforts *not* to hurt her were doing even more damage.

I pleaded with her. I promised Alyssa that I could change. I promised we could go to a counselor together. I wept and begged and swore. Each time I reached for her hand, Alyssa flinched and pulled farther away. We went on like that all evening, until there was nothing left to say. She wanted me out by the end of the month. She'd already contacted a lawyer and paid a deposit (her parents had lent her the money). At least we didn't have any kids. Hell, we didn't even have a dog or a cat to fight over. There was just us, and soon enough, there wouldn't even be that anymore.

"Why are you doing this?" I asked her, as she walked me to the door.

"I'm doing what I have to do to survive, Pete. Isn't that what you always say? Do what you have to do to survive?"

I couldn't respond to her because there was nothing I could say. Alyssa was right. Many times since then, I'd played the conversation back in my head, searching for things I could have said, different words or promises that might have changed the outcome, but there are none. I know that now.

Things are how they are. It is what it is. You do what you have to do to survive. And if the situation changes, and life throws you a curveball, then you'd better well fucking adapt.

Adapt or die.

Things didn't work out with Hannah. Distraught over the divorce and riding an emotional rollercoaster, I'd shown up drunk at her apartment, crying in the rain. She'd invited me inside and dried me off, and when I told her what had happened, she'd done her best to console me. We ended up having sex. I can't call it making love, because it was anything but that. It was just sex. I lay there in the darkness after it was over, shivering and thinking about Alyssa. Her words, her accusations—her truths—echoed in my head. I turned over, looked at Hannah, and told her it had been a mistake. Then I got dressed while she sat there in the bed, a sheet wrapped around her breasts, staring at me with hurt and confusion. She asked me to stay, and I told her that I couldn't. I told her we'd talk about it more later, but we never did. I went out of my way to avoid her at work. I stopped taking her phone calls and blocked her email address. Two weeks later, she quit the Pocahontas. I don't know what happened to her after that. I'd like to think she found someone who treated her the way she deserved, and that she was happy, if even for a brief while before the world ended—but I just don't know.

I don't know what happened to Alyssa either, ultimately. Since becoming trapped in the bunker, I'd tried not to let myself dwell on the possibilities—whether she was still alive somewhere out there, or had instead joined the ranks of the walking dead. In either case, she was gone. Out of reach. In truth, I'd lost her long before the zombies came. Our story was over before this one began. A good friend of mine had told me—shortly after Alyssa and I split up—that divorce was like a death without a corpse, and that I had to grieve and mourn just like I'd have had to do if she'd died.

Thinking too much about Alyssa's possible fate only led to more heartbreak and frustration. Late at night, I told myself that she'd escaped. I imagined her somewhere else, maybe in a police station or an Army base or maybe on a boat, out to sea and out of the zombies' reach. I imagined her happy and alive, and maybe missing me. Somehow, that made my sense of loss much more profound.

***

I sat there in the incinerator room, overwhelmed with remorse, battered by my guilty conscience and sick to my stomach over everything from the way I'd treated Alyssa to the murder I'd just committed, and wondered again why I even bothered. What was the point in all this? Why keep struggling, trapped beneath a mountain with a bunch of madmen and slowly starving to death? Why not just end it all right now? Just start the incinerator up and climb inside, or poke my head outside and offer myself up as a snack to the zombies. Not that I'd be much of a meal for them, not with all the weight I'd lost.

I thought about the people we'd lost in the first few days of the siege—folks like Annie Leavell, a very kind, generous and gregarious woman who had worked in one of the Pocahontas's shops and had passed away from a heart attack on our third day here, and Ryan Burack, a tourist from Wisconsin who'd been staying in the hotel when the shit hit the fan and died our first night in the bunker, passing quietly in his sleep. We never figured out the cause. We hadn't even known Ryan's name until we pulled out his wallet after his death. We knew that Annie had a daughter, Chesya, who she'd talked about all the time. It felt wrong, not being able to inform her daughter of her death.

We'd put Annie and Ryan and all the others into the incinerator, because it was the only way to dispose of their bodies. It had been a solemn, if gruesome task. We'd treated them with respect—offered words of peace and mumbled prayers before we sent them on their way, reducing them to ashes. Had they been the lucky ones? Annie had, quite literally, died laughing. At least she'd gone out relatively happy, despite the circumstances. At least she hadn't died on an empty stomach. Would I be able to say the same? At that point, it seemed like it would be a lot easier just to give up and give in.

But I didn't. I didn't think about it. I didn't have to. It was instinct. Pure, primal instinct. When Chuck and the others knocked on the door a moment later, I forgot all about Alyssa and Annie all of the things that had gone wrong in my life, and went right back to doing what I had to do to survive.

FOUR

"Pete?"

I held my breath. My heart pounded in my throat and I heard my blood rushing through my ears.

"Open up, Pete."

It was Chuck. I recognized his voice, even through the thick walls. The door clanged as something hard and metallic was rapped against it. The sound repeated once. Twice. Then Chuck called out again.

"We know you're in there, Pete. Come on out."

I didn't say anything. I scrambled to my feet and quietly moved away from the door. I clenched my fists so hard that my fingernails dug deep into my palms.

The knocking returned, this time faster and with more force. It stopped suddenly, followed by a muffled, angry curse.

"Come on, Pete. It doesn't have to be this way. We can talk about it if you want. I don't know what Drew told you, but—"

"Save it, Chuck." My eyes widened in surprise. I hadn't meant to speak out loud. Then, deciding the damage had already been done, I continued. "Drew told me exactly what's going on. Even if he hadn't, Krantz sure as fuck verified it for me. Have you lost your goddamned mind?"

"Me?" Chuck sounded genuinely offended. "You're the one whose lost his mind, Pete. You killed Krantz."

"Only because he would have killed me. It was self defense."

"That's not true," someone else shouted. I couldn't tell who they were for sure. A male, certainly, but the speaker could have been one of many people.

"Shut up," Chuck told the other person, loud enough that I could hear him through the door. There was a moment of silence and then Chuck spoke again. His tone had changed, his voice now tinged with anger and annoyance. I was messing up his plans. I wasn't going along with the group vote. I was making him look bad in front of the others. The thought made me grin.

"Let's face facts here, Pete. You're unarmed and alone and trapped in there with no other way out. There's more of us than there are of you. It's over. You know that. Face it like a man. Come on out."

"Fuck you. I'm staying right here."

"Pete, you—"

"Did I stutter, Chuck? Go fuck yourself."

"I know it's not easy, but you need to face facts. None of us likes this. You think we're animals or something? Of course we aren't. We didn't come down here just to turn into cannibals, man. But that's the hand we've been dealt. If it's any consolation, I didn't want it to go down this way. Drew sort of ruined everything by telling you. I swear, we meant to take you in your sleep. You wouldn't have felt a thing. You wouldn't have even known."

"That's very kind of you." I said it loud enough so that he could hear me through the door, hoping to distract him and keep him talking long enough for me to escape. Chuck was right about one thing. I was outnumbered and overwhelmed. I didn't know how many people he had out there with him, but even if it was just three of them, I'd have a problem defending myself in this small space, with only a fire extinguisher and my fists to use as weapons. Hunger had physically weakened all of us, but three against one was bad odds no matter how strong a person was.

"We're coming in now," Chuck said. "My advice to you is to not fight it. You'll only make things harder on yourself. I give you my word that this can happen peacefully. You won't even be aware of it. We've got enough painkillers and stuff that you can still go in your sleep. We can knock you out. But if you want to go hard, Pete, then so be it."

"Come on in," I challenged, raising my eyes toward the ductwork above me. "See what happens."

There was another brief pause and then the iron bar wiggled as they tried to open the door from the other side. My blockade held fast. The door didn't budge. It thudded as something was forced against it from the other side. Then I heard somebody groan as if in pain.

"It's locked, and now I hurt my damned shoulder."

I recognized this speaker as a man named Phillips. I didn't know much about him, other than he had been a sales rep for some kind of foam insulation company, and he'd been here on vacation when the zombies attacked. His wife and kids had apparently been topside when the zombies attacked, and hadn't made it down into the bunker with him, but Phillips had never seemed too upset about that. I hadn't liked him very much to begin with, and the fact that he was now intent on joining in with the others to murder and eat me didn't improve my disposition toward him.

"Try it again," Chuck ordered.

The iron bar rattled as they hammered on the door, but once more held fast. Blows resounded through the small room as they hit the door faster and harder. Their curses grew louder. I heard Chuck tell someone to get the cutting torch. Two acetylene torches had been left down here by a maintenance crew before the siege. We'd held onto them, like everything else in the bunker. Drew had mentioned at the time that we could always use them to cut our way out of the bunker, should the blast doors become inoperable. I'd had my doubts about that. The cutting torches weren't powerful enough to cut through twelve feet of solid steel.

The blows on the door intensified. Then they suddenly ceased. I heard the sound of squeaking wheels, like a cart being hauled down the hallway. Then another man shouted. I recognized the voice as that of Jim Mars, one of the many who had urged me not to wait for Mike when this whole thing started and the zombies attacked. I'd liked him up until now. He'd been kind and soft-spoken and talked a lot about his wife and kids and how he hoped they were still alive. When we'd started to run low on food, Mars had always been willing to share his with others. He'd joked that he needed to lose weight anyway. Apparently, he'd since changed his mind about that, seeing as how he was with Chuck and the rest of the group on the other side of the door.

"Here," he yelled. "I've got the torch!"

"Fire it up," Chuck said. I'm certain he raised his voice so that I'd hear him.

Trying to move as quietly as possible, I opened the incinerator door and peered inside. The interior was full of ashes and darkness, and smelled *heavy*. There was no other way to describe it—just a thick, weighty odor. I stuck my head inside and gazed up into the shadows. At the top was the drop chute which led to the shower room one floor above us. Designed so that survivors of a nuclear war could dispose of their irradiated clothing, it was now my best—and probably only—chance at escape.

I hunched down and climbed inside the incinerator. It was big enough inside for me to crouch on my hands and knees, but doing so stirred up clouds of swirling dust, which got into my throat and sinuses. I wondered how much of it was the ashes of the people we'd burned in there. Was I inhaling Annie? Coughing, I made my way toward the chute. Something crunched under my feet. I looked down and saw that it was a half-charred bone. I wondered whose it had been. Outside, I heard the hiss of an acetylene torch being lit, and moments later, the room began to fill with the stench of scorched metal. It was strong enough that I could smell it over the odor of the incinerator. I reached out, grabbed the incinerator door, and pulled it shut behind me.

"Won't be long now, Pete," Chuck hollered. His voice was muffled. "You'll be sorry you made us do this."

"Not half as sorry as you're going to be."

Even though I'd whispered, my voice seemed to echo in the shaft. I pressed my back against one wall and my knees against the other, and then wriggled up the chute like a snake, hoping that there was nobody waiting for me on the other side. I moved quickly but as quietly as possible, fearful that Chuck and the others would hear me through the ductwork and discover what I was doing, despite the noise they were making. The inside of the shaft was black with soot, and I focused on breathing through my mouth, choking off sneezes that would have certainly given away my position. My eyes watered and my throat felt raw and scratchy. My breath began to sound harsh and loud, and I wondered if they could hear it echoing through the shaft. The chute narrowed and the walls began to feel like they were closing in on me. Sweat beaded on my forehead and cheeks, and stung my eyes. I tried blinking it away, but to no avail. My eyes watered and my vision blurred. The cloying smell from the cutting torch grew stronger, even inside the shaft. My muscles began to cramp, but I pushed on, determined to get away.

When I reached the top, I paused at the chute door and listened. I was far enough up that the sounds from below had faded, and although I could still smell burning metal, the stench wasn't as overpowering. I didn't hear anything from the shower room, and was fairly certain it was unoccupied, but I was still concerned that Chuck and the others would be able to hear me through the ductwork. By this point, the pain in my muscles and joints had grown excruciating. My body was starting to tremble and my vision was blurred to the point of blindness. I opened the chute door very slowly. When there was no reaction, I thrust my head through the opening. The air in the empty shower room felt cool upon my face, and I sighed with relief. Wiping the stinging sweat from my eyes, I slowly crawled out of the chute and plopped down onto the floor. A quick glance around confirmed that I was alone. Either the searchers hadn't reached this level yet, or my escape hadn't been discovered. I wondered how long it would take them to cut through the door to the incinerator room. At least a few more minutes, judging by how long it had taken me to climb up the chute. That bought me a little precious time, but once they'd broken into the room and figured out where I'd gone, that time would run out. Despite the danger, I sat there for a few moments until I'd caught my breath and the pain in my muscles had subsided. Then I scrambled to my feet and tried to figure out what the hell to do next.

The shower room was a small, ugly space. It smelled faintly of mildew and unidentifiable chemicals, despite the fact that the hotel staff (myself included) had cleaned it once a week ever since tours of the bunker began. The showers themselves had been disconnected years ago—the pipes and plumbing cut off. Now they were just exhibits. There had been rumors among some of the employees that the room was haunted. Supposedly, people occasionally heard the phantom sound of water dripping, or heard disembodied footsteps. Once, a tourist from Wisconsin asked her tour guide who the little girl standing under one of the shower nozzles was. When the tour guide didn't see anyone there, the tourist had insisted that she'd seen a little girl. I don't know if there was really a ghost or not, although it occurred to me that if I didn't think of something quick, my spirit stood a good chance of haunting these halls. Maybe we all would—a different kind of dead from the ones outside. Ghosts, rather than zombies, our spirits haunting those who had experienced a different kind of life after death. The thought gave me chills. My skin prickled.

Personally, I never saw or heard anything weird in the shower room—unless you count the drunken tourist who passed out in there once and cracked his head open when he fell—but the décor alone was enough to give me the creeps. The walls, floor and ceiling were covered in small, faded-yellow tiles, many of which were cracked or chipped. The overhead lights were weak, and their radiance had always seemed washed-out and sickly to me. The space was devoid of furnishing, except for the showerheads, a drain in the slightly-sloped floor, and the burn chute from which I'd just climbed out of. A rack was affixed to one wall. It displayed several coarse brooms and brushes, which would have been used to scrub any irradiated survivors upon their admission into the bunker. On the floor beneath it sat an empty canister of delousing agent. The brooms and the canister were nothing more than museum pieces now. I'd gestured to them a hundred times while giving tours, droning on monotonously about their intended usage while secretly wishing the work day was over so I could get home to Alyssa. It had never occurred to me at the time that I'd one day be using them as weapons, but that's exactly what I did next. I grabbed one of the brooms from the rack, twisted off the broom itself, and then snapped the handle down over my knee. I was weak enough from hunger that I had to do this three times before the handle snapped, and I got a big, purple bruise on my knee in the process. I stared at the jagged lengths in my hand. Now I had two spears. They were crude, yes, but they were better than nothing, and if Chuck and the others weren't armed, they might make all the difference. Just holding them made me feel better and more confident. My panic subsided a bit, and I paused long enough to consider my options.

The shower room had one exit, an open doorway that led directly into the decontamination center, which, while a much larger space, had the same depressing décor as the shower area. The only difference is the tiles were blue rather than piss-yellow. Like much of the rest of the bunker, the decontamination center had been left as is in order to show visitors what it would have been like if operational. That appearance could be summed up in one word—boring. The only furnishings was an empty metal desk, a chair, and a row of rusty, gunmetal-gray filing cabinets, all of which were also empty. At one point, the lower drawer in the farthermost left filing cabinet had contained one of my fellow tour guides' vintage porn magazine collection, but that had been discovered by my fellow survivors weeks ago and promptly disseminated—complete with pages stuck together from previous viewings. I didn't care. Having come of age by looking at porn on the internet, the magazines had always struck me as kind of kitschy. They were something my father would have looked at.

My thoughts turned to him. He'd been gone four years now. He'd suffered a massive and sudden brain hemorrhage while mowing the lawn. Both my mother and myself had always been after him to let me do it, but my father had vehemently declined all offers of assistance. My grandfather had been the same way. At the age of ninety, he'd climbed a ladder and replaced some missing tiles on his roof, adamant that he could still do it himself—and he had. My parents had put him in a home soon after, which had broken his heart. It broke my parents' hearts, too. My mother had passed on two years after my father, after a short battle with advanced lymphoma that hadn't been caught in time. In her final years, she'd fervently hoped that Alyssa and I would give her a grandbaby. We never did, though, and I was glad for that now, for a number of reasons, the first and foremost of which was the zombies. Who in their right mind would bring a kid into this shit? I was glad that my parents and my grandfather weren't around anymore. The state of the world would have broken their hearts more than the old folks home or the lack of a grandbaby ever had.

For a brief moment, I considered trying to unscrew one of the metal legs from the desk, but I decided against it. I didn't have any tools and attempting to do it with my fingers would take too much time. What I needed to do was find some place safe to hide out, and then I could plan my next move. Surrender was out of the question, but fighting everyone in the bunker didn't seem like a realistic option, either, especially when armed only with a broken broom handle.

The decontamination center had a small restroom that was still functional. We'd kept it closed and off limits to tour groups, but me and the other guides had still used it from time to time, mostly to sneak a cigarette or when we had to go really bad and wouldn't be able to wait until we'd reached the other side of the bunker, where the public restrooms were. The door to the restroom was open, and although the light was off inside, I was certain there was nobody hiding in there and waiting for me. I ducked inside, knelt, and raised the toilet seat. Then I cupped my hands, dipped them into the water, and took several deep draughts. I wasn't grossed out by the thought of drinking from the toilet. I'd long since given up caring about such civilized niceties. Besides, dogs drank out of toilets, and dogs were the best creatures on the planet. The only thing I did mind was the room-temperature water's faint chemical taste. I grimaced as I drank. I gorged myself, unsure of when I'd be able to drink again. Who knew how long I'd have to be in hiding, or how Drew would find me—if he was even alive to find me. I felt very guilty over the possibility that Drew might pay the price for my actions, but that didn't stop me from continuing on. I splashed some water on my face and then stood up.

It was at that point that I noticed the sink. I mean, I'd known it was there before, but for some reason, my mind had totally blanked out, and I'd gone to the toilet instead. A brain fart, Drew would have called it. I chalked it up to fear and stress.

Both were weighing on me. My mind had just had a little blip. That was all. After wiping my face and hands with some paper towels, I left the restroom and looked for a place to hide.

I emerged into another hallway and found myself at a crossroads. If I went left, I'd walk down a gray concrete four-hundred and thirty-three foot long tunnel that led to a dead end—the bunker's mountainside blast door. A right turn would take me deeper into the bunker via the facility's sprawling power plant, which was still operational. I could hear the distant roar of the power plant's generators from where I stood. Beyond the power plant was a stairwell that led down to the lower level, where Chuck and the others were. I didn't want to risk running into them, so I turned left and hurried down the tunnel. I walked briskly at first, but then panic took over and I broke into a jog. My shoes slapped against the concrete. The sounds echoed off the walls, and I hoped the hum of the generators would drown them out.

I caught a whiff of myself as I ran. The smell made me grimace. I stank—the unfortunate effect of weeks without showering or washing my clothes, with the added effect of the ketosis ravaging my starved body, and the puke I'd spewed all over myself in the incinerator room. My faded jeans, long-sleeved black shirt, socks, and boxer-briefs with various DC Comics superheroes on them were all stiff enough to stand up by themselves. My hair felt stiff, too, long past the point of just being greasy. The whiskers on my face itched and made my skin sore. I'd never had a beard until we came underground. I'd washed in the sink as often as possible, but that didn't really get me clean. We'd gone through the restroom's meager supply of hand soap in the first week, and other than some bottle of hand sanitizer, none of us had any other soaps or cleaners on us when we got stuck down here. I longed for many things—food, a decent night's sleep, toothpaste, a cold beer, someone to hold—but more than any of these things, with the possible exception of food, what I wanted most was to take a hot shower. I wanted to stand under a scalding, forceful stream of water and just close my eyes and not move.

Right after I ate something, of course.

The corridor seemed to stretch out before me, as if the end was racing ahead, always out of reach. I'd walked it so many times, but it had never seemed longer than it did at that moment. It was silent, save for my echoing footsteps and the background noise from the power plant. The overhead lights glowed brightly, casting their stark, fluorescent radiance over everything. There were no shadows to hide in. No dark corners to duck into. The gray concrete walls were featureless except for stenciled signs advising me of where the exit was located. Water supply pipes ran overhead, along with ductwork and electrical conduits. There were several sewer grates in the floor. I paused over one, debating whether to duck down into the sewer and hide out there, and then decided against it. I'd choose that as a last resort.

As I approached the end of the tunnel, the blast door loomed into view. There was a small cul-de-sac to the left, right before the tunnel terminated at the door. Parked inside this little nook were two old forklifts, leftovers from when the bunker had been an active site. The hotel had inherited them and they'd sat here ever since. Occasionally, one of the maintenance staff would hop on one and ride it around, but they were only really used when it came to changing the fluorescent lights overhead. One worker would stand on the forks, balanced precariously along with a case of light bulbs, while his co-worker would raise the forks up to the ceiling. One forklift was a bright orange Toyota model. The other was a yellow Caterpillar. Both operated on propane, and both had full canisters strapped behind them. My fellow survivors had only used them once since the siege had started—Chuck had suggested a forklift race to break the monotony after several weeks. It had sufficed, until the exhaust fumes building up in the tunnel had started to make us sick.

Stacked behind the forklifts were three diesel generators, each still sitting on a skid and wrapped with plastic. Another skid was stacked with boxes of replacement fluorescent bulbs. A metal rack held a few spare propane bottles for the forklifts. Hanging on the wall next to it was a fire extinguisher. Although the lighting in the cul-de-sac was just as bright as the rest of the tunnel, there was a shadowy area between the wall and the skids. If I needed to, I could hide there. Chances were I'd be discovered if anyone approached closely, though.

"Maybe the zombies aren't out there anymore," I whispered. "Maybe they've moved on. Maybe I can sneak out right now before anyone finds me."

Even as I said it, I knew I'd be wrong. It was wishful thinking, and nothing more. I might as well have said, "Maybe aliens will arrive and take me to the lost planet of Nibiru, which is populated by Sports Illustrated swimsuit models." Sighing, I turned my attention to the blast door. Mounted on the wall overhead was a closed circuit television monitor. Since we still had power, the unit was still functioning. I stared at the grainy, washed out black and white image. Hundreds of dead milled around the door, pawing at the entrance. Most of them looked like they'd been out there a while. The ones closest to the door were in bad shape. One particularly fermented corpse seemed to be stuck to the door, as if the sun had melted him onto it like the syrupy remains of a popsicle left out in the sun on a sidewalk. Insects crawled all over—and through—him. Many of the zombies were missing limbs. One had been completely hollowed. The decay and damage were so bad that I couldn't tell if it was a man or a woman. All that remained of them from the neck down to their waistline was an empty, gaping cavity. Several zombie animals were in the group, as well. The most grotesque of all was a severed head. I caught a glimpse of it as the corpses momentarily parted. Its blackened tongue protruded from its mouth, and its eyes moved back and forth, desperately seeking prey even though it could no longer hunt.

Suddenly, I was overwhelmed with a desire to be outside with them. The urge was so strong that I had to stop myself from reaching for the wheel to open the door. On the other side of that impregnable steel was the sky and fresh air and green trees and grass. I wanted so badly to experience those things again. I wanted to feel the sun's warmth on my skin, or to stand beneath the shade of a tree as the leaves rustled softly above me. I wanted to smell fresh-cut grass and honeysuckle and pines. I wanted to hear birds chirping and squirrels chattering at one another. I wanted to feel the wind. To taste it. To hear it. Hell, I'd have been ecstatic just to feel the bite of a mosquito or to hear the buzz of a bumblebee. All I had was the sounds of the bunker, and after being cooped up down here, those sounds had left me demoralized and depressed—and apparently, they'd driven my fellow survivors crazy.

On the screen, a human zombie repeatedly slapped the door with a severed penis he clutched in his fist. A dead dog licked the steel, slowly and methodically, as if trying to wear down the door with its tongue. Another zombie's eyeball popped in its socket as I watched. The gooey remnants slipped down the corpse's cheek like a squashed grey slug. A cloud of flies swarmed toward the hole and began to crawl in and out. Disgusted by what I was watching, yet strangely compelled to watch it anyway, I shuffled toward the blast door, my peril momentarily forgotten. I was thankful that the closed circuit system had no sound. Seeing them was one thing. Hearing them was another, and smelling them was even worse. As I got close to the door, I imagined that I could hear them. Despite the background noise from the power plant and the unbelievable thickness of the door itself, I heard their distant moans. The dead sounded hungry.

I knew how they felt. My stomach grumbled, as if in sympathy, and I clutched at it through my shirt, feeling my ribs beneath the fabric. I tried to remember how long it had been since I'd eaten, and found that I couldn't. In truth, I couldn't even remember the last time I'd taken a shit. I hadn't needed to for a while. There was nothing inside of me that had needed to come out, other than piss and despair and madness, and I'd been doing a pretty good job of keeping that last one bottled up.

Still holding my stomach, I returned to the cul-de-sac, climbed over the skids, and ducked down behind them. I laid one of my makeshift spears on the floor and clutched the other one in my fist. After laying it across my lap, I leaned back and tried to lose myself in the shadows. I settled in to wait for someone to show.

It turned out that I didn't have to wait for long.

FIVE

"Careful now. He could be hiding underneath one of those forklifts."

I snorted, coming fully awake, and sat up so quickly that I banged the back of my head against the wall. I winced, barely keeping from crying out. My eyes watered as I rubbed my head. Then I held still and listened. My pulse raced from zero to ninety. I was certain someone had heard me.

"Is that true, Pete?" The speaker was a man, but I couldn't tell who. It was hard to judge how far away he was, due to the tunnel's echoing effects. "You hiding out over there?"

Their footsteps drew closer. I could hear them even over the distant sounds from the power plant, which meant that they were close by. I cursed myself for falling asleep. How had I allowed that to happen, and perhaps more importantly, how long had I been out? Did they know I was here? Judging by their conversation, it didn't seem that way, but what if they were just toying with me? Trying to psyche me out? I glanced down. One of my spears was still on my lap and the other lay out of reach. It must have rolled away while I slept. I grabbed the one in my lap, gripping the shaft so tightly that my knuckles turned white. I wanted to sit up the entire way and peer out over the skids, but I resisted the urge. My only hope at that moment was that the shadows would conceal me. If they actually entered the cul-de-sac and looked over the forklifts and generators, I'd be caught. I took a deep breath and held it. The footsteps stopped.

"See anything?" I recognized the speaker as George Laidlaw, a fellow employee of the Pocahontas and up until this point, a fairly decent guy.

"No." I knew that soft-spoken voice, as well. It was Jim Mars. "Ain't nothing here."

"He could be behind those skids." A third speaker. Male, and judging from the accent, a local, but I still didn't recognize the voice.

"Pete," Jim called, "come on out if you're there. I don't like it any more than you do, but there's no helping it. Come on out. You're only making this harder on yourself."

My nose suddenly began to itch. I resisted the urge to move. When my stomach gurgled, I thought for sure they had heard it.

"Go on back there," George said. "Let's make sure."

"He ain't there," the unidentified third man said. "I still say he's probably hiding out in the power plant. That's sure as hell where I'd go if it was me."

"Well, it ain't you."

"I'm just saying, is all."

"And I said we need to make sure, Clyde."

I silently thanked George for filling me in on the third man's identity. It was Clyde Osborne, a shifty little runt from Punkin Center who worked at the hotel as a greens keeper. 'Worked' was a relative term, since all Clyde had ever seemed to do was take smoke breaks. He'd weighed about a buck oh five before we ran out of food, and weeks of starvation hadn't improved his condition. He'd be no problem, if it came to a fight.

"Come on," Jim said. "The sooner we get this over with, the better. My stomach is in knots. This don't sit well with me."

The footsteps shuffled closer and there was a subtle change in the lighting. Without turning my head, I looked to the right and saw shadows on the wall. Whoever it was, they were close enough that I could hear them breathing. I closed my eyes and gritted my teeth. My entire body tensed.

"Got him," Clyde shouted. "He's hunkered down back here behind this—"

Without thinking, I jumped up from my hiding place and thrust the spear at him. The jagged point stabbed the fleshy part of his shoulder, right between his arm and his chest. There was a brief second of resistance and then the spear sank into his skin. Clyde wailed. I heard the other two men holler. Something slipped from Clyde's hand and clattered onto the floor. I glanced down and saw that it was a length of pipe that he'd apparently intended to use as a club.

"Goddamn," he screamed. "The fucker stabbed me."

Jim and George stood just outside the cul-de-sac, gaping at us both. George was armed with a pocketknife. Jim had a piece of two-by-four. On the closed circuit television, the zombies seemed to be watching the action, as well. I wondered if they could sense the struggle going on beneath the mountain. Grunting, I yanked my spear free. Clyde stumbled backward, his free hand pressing against his wound. Blood welled from between his fingers. I thrust the spear at him and he scrambled away. He bumped against the nearest forklift and fell down. Despite everything, I laughed. At first, the noise confused me. I wasn't aware that it was me making the sound. Then I saw the panic in Clyde's wide eyes, and I laughed harder. I lifted my head and stared at Jim and George.

"Who's next? How about you, George? You want some?"

"Fuck you," George said quietly.

"No, fuck you, you cocksucker. It doesn't have to be this way, George. None of this has to happen. I mean, have you guys stopped for just one second and thought about what you're doing here?"

Jim sighed. "You killed Krantz, Pete."

"Because you guys were going to kill me. It was self-defense, man."

"So is this."

I groaned with frustration. "Are you really so far gone that Chuck's idea seems like a good one?"

"It's better than starving to death," George said.

Jim nodded in agreement. "I want to make it back home to my family, Pete."

"I don't think that's going to happen anytime soon."

He shook his head. "Sooner or later, the zombies will go away. They're rotting. Eventually, there won't be anything left of them. We're just waiting for the last zombie."

"That might take a while."

"I'll wait. Sooner or later they'll be none left. When that happens, I've got to get home to my family. With the zombies gone, there won't be any law or order. I've got to protect my family from what comes next. I'm no good to them if I'm dead."

"You've got no family to go home to!" Spittle flew from my lips. "If they were outside, then they're as good as dead already. Don't you see that?"

Jim flinched, and took a faltering step backward, as if I'd physically slapped him. When he spoke again, his voice was barely a whisper.

"That's not true. It's not true. We have a basement. They probably hid down there. I'm sure of it. They—"

"They're dead," I insisted. "I'm sorry for your loss, but you've got to face the facts. They're gone, and you can't get them back again."

On the floor, Clyde moaned. I lashed out with my foot and kicked him.

"Shut up."

"You stabbed me, you fucker."

"You're damned right I did, and I'll do it again if you don't shut up." I turned my attention back to Jim and George. "It's time we take a good, hard look at reality. We need to focus on ourselves. Everyone we love is probably dead. They're probably walking around like the rest of those things outside."

"That may be true," George said, "but we're dead, too, if we don't eat something soon. I'm not saying Chuck's plan is right or decent or moral, but *it is necessary*, Pete. You just had the bad luck of being the first to be chosen. If it's any consolation, I'm sorry about how things turned out. We all are."

I snorted. "Yeah, you seem real choked up about it, George. You're a real humanitarian."

He shrugged. "Believe me or not. It's the truth. I puked twice on the way up here. I ain't no killer, but I'll do what I have to do. We all will."

"And what about after I'm gone? Huh? What then, George? What are you guys going to do when there's nothing left of me but bones?"

"Well, then we'll put you in the incinerator, I guess."

"That's not what I mean. Eventually, you'll get hungry again. You'll have to pick someone else. What if it's you, the next time? Or you, Jim? Or you, Clyde? What then? You'll be standing in the same place where I'm standing now. Is it still going to be okay then? Come on, guys. I know things are bad, but this isn't the way."

"Do you have a better idea? One that doesn't involve going outside and getting overwhelmed by the zombies? Because if so, then I'm all ears."

"No," I admitted, my voice faltering. "I don't. But even if you go along with Chuck's plan, how long do you think I'd last, once you killed me? How long before I'm inedible? A day? Two? Let's get real—we're talking about meat. We've got no way to preserve it. You'd have to kill somebody again pretty damn quick."

"There's a refrigerator in the kitchen," George said. "One of those big stainless steel jobs like the kind you find in restaurants. I know it's just part of the exhibit, but it still works. I reckon we can keep you fresh a lot longer than two days."

I paused before responding. I felt sort of stunned. I'd forgotten all about the refrigerator. I suddenly had an image of my various organs and body parts sealed inside of Tupperware containers and stuffed into the vegetable crisper drawers.

"What if the power goes out?" I asked. "What happens then? The diesel fuel won't last forever. One of the generators could break down."

George shrugged. "If the power goes out, then we'll smoke you. Charles Smith thinks we can set something up in the incinerator room to do just that."

"You're insane."

"No," George replied, "I'm not crazy. I'm just hungry. I'm hungry and I want to live. I'm sorry about this, Pete. I really am. You were a nice guy. You don't deserve this. But I want to live. We all do. This isn't personal. This is just the way it has to be. I want to live, and if killing you makes that happen, then so be it. Now, are you gonna come out of there like a man, or are we going to have to come get you and drag you out?"

"Don't do this," I begged, hating the plaintive tone in my voice. "Please…"

They both charged me at the same time, as if responding to some unspoken signal. Jim came in from the left, his makeshift club held at arm's length like a baseball bat. George moved slower, more stealthily, creeping forward with the pocketknife at the ready. I raised the spear to meet Jim's attack, and moved toward him, but Clyde reached out from the floor and grabbed my ankle. His fingers were warm and sticky with his blood. I could feel it through my sock. Repulsed, I jerked my foot from his grasp and kicked him hard in the chin. I heard his teeth clack together as he hurtled backward. Clyde uttered a garbled scream as blood rushed from his mouth. I remember thinking that there seemed to be a lot of it—too much blood for what I'd just done, but then Jim was upon me. He lashed out with his club, swinging hard and grunting with the effort. It was the grunt that saved me. I managed to step backward, narrowly avoiding the blow. I jabbed my spear at him, but he sidestepped it. Jim was breathing heavy. His mouth hung slack and his eyes seemed tired and unfocused. He raised his weapon to swing again, and I thrust my spear into his armpit and shoved hard. It sank in like a knife cutting through a block of cheese. Jim opened his mouth. Whether to speak or cry out, I don't know, because all he managed to do was wheeze. His knees bent. He reached behind him, frowning in confusion, and then toppled backward, taking my spear with him.

Weaponless, I stood there as George closed in on me. He moved silently, stepping over Jim's body without even glancing down at it. He didn't speak. I wasn't even sure if he was breathing. If it hadn't been for the grim determination showing in his eyes or the tiny muscle twitching in his cheek, I might have thought he was a zombie. He approached with caution, but his steps didn't falter. He moved in a sort of crouch, head ducked low, arms pulled in tight to his body, knife at the ready.

"It doesn't have to be like this," I told him. "There's still time, George. Put the knife down."

He didn't answer, nor did he pause. He continued toward

me, and now his determined expression had been replaced with a look of something else.

Hunger.

George was hungry. Hell, he wasn't just hungry. He was ravenous. I noticed for the first time the thin line of drool leaking from the corner of his mouth. In that moment, he wasn't a man at all. Instead, he reminded me of an animal. George was something primal and savage. He was a hunter.

And I was the prey.

At that moment, I felt a fear unlike anything I'd felt before. It was stronger than what I'd experienced in the movie room and more powerful than the day Alyssa left me. I imagined this was how a squirrel felt as it watched the headlights of an onrushing car. I stumbled away, hoping to reach my other spear, which was still lying on the floor behind the skid. Before I could, George seized my flapping shirttail and lunged at me. My fear dissolved into panic, consuming me. I didn't think. I just acted. The sounds I made didn't seem like my own—a long, keening scream that had no words. I punched and kicked and screamed, lashing out with my fists and feet, biting and head-butting and doing anything I could just to prevent the inevitable—just to stay alive for one second longer. All sound ceased. I was dimly aware that I was still screaming, but I couldn't hear it. I couldn't see, either. Everything in the cul-de-sac, including George, became a blur. I remained in motion, delivering blow after blow, not knowing if they were connecting or not—and not really caring if they did. The important thing was to not stop.

Eventually, I did stop. The first thing I became aware of was the sound of my own breathing. I was hyperventilating. My arms hung limp at my sides, and my shoulders sagged. The floor seemed spongy and uneven, and my feet felt wet and sticky. When I glanced down with half-open eyes, I saw why. I was standing on top of what was left of George. At first, I didn't recognize him. Both of his eyes were blackish-purple and swollen shut. His lips were split and swollen, too, and his nose resembled a squashed kiwi fruit. There was a hole in his cheek—a ragged, raw wound that looked *chewed*. Blood leaked from his nose and ears and the corners of his eyes. It covered the front of his shirt and had dribbled down his neck. I stared at him in confusion, wondering what had happened. Then I realized that it was *me* that had happened to him. *I* had done this. I'd killed him.

My fists were still clenched. I uncurled them, wincing with pain as I did. The knuckles on both hands were sore and bloody, and the middle finger on my left hand was starting to swell. There were cuts on my hands from George's teeth. I licked my lips and tasted blood. At first, I thought it was mine, but it wasn't. I'd bitten that hole in George's cheek. I spat, wiping my mouth with my forearm. It hurt to breathe. My chest ached. I checked myself thoroughly to make sure George hadn't stabbed or cut me. Other than the lacerations on my hands, I didn't seem to be injured, though my shirt was torn.

I looked around for the pocketknife, but couldn't find it. I assumed it must have been tossed aside during the fight. I got down on my hands and knees, searching for it. I found the weapon lying beneath one of the diesel generators. It had slipped beneath the skid and the plastic sheeting surrounding the unit. I pulled it free, closed the blade and slipped the knife into my pocket. Then I checked the bodies, just to make sure the three of them were dead. George wasn't breathing, and neither was Jim. In the case of the latter, it was obvious what had killed him, but despite the obvious physical damage to George, I couldn't believe that my beating alone had killed him. When I rolled him over, I saw that it hadn't. The back of his head was cracked open and his hair was matted and sticky with fresh blood. He must have hit his head on the concrete when he fell. Clyde was bloodier than both Jim and George. He'd bitten the tip of his tongue off when I'd kicked him in the chin. I looked around for it, but didn't see it anywhere, so I assumed he swallowed it. Maybe he'd choked on it, or maybe he'd bled to death. I couldn't be sure—but then again, it didn't really matter, as long as he was dead and not trying to eat me anymore.

A thought occurred to me then. There was no reason why

Chuck and the others had to continue hunting me. If it was food they needed—if they were determined to offset starvation by eating our fellow survivors—then I'd actually done them a favor. Why hadn't I thought of this before, when I killed Krantz? They could eat him instead. And with the bodies of George, Jim and Clyde, it was like a four-course meal. There would be enough to feed everyone.

I tried freeing my spear from inside of Jim, but it was stuck on something. I didn't want to consider what might be obstructing it—bone, probably. Maybe one of his ribs? Each time I tugged on the shaft, another gout of blood bubbled out of his mouth. He'd shit and pissed himself in death, and when I jiggled the spear, his body moved, making wet, squelching sounds. The stench was atrocious. Finally, I gave up and retrieved the second spear from where it lay. Then, gripping it in my hand, I stepped over their corpses and peeked around the cul-de-sac wall.

The corridor was empty and quiet. The only sound was the ever-present rumbling of the generators in the power plant. I decided that I was sick of skulking around and hiding. There was no sense in it anymore, given that the others were dead. All I had to do was explain it to Chuck and his followers. I stretched, turning my head from side to side and cracking my joints. Then I walked down the hall, spear in hand. The lights seemed brighter than before, and the corridor seemed even longer. As the adrenalin left my body, my stomach began to ache again.

All of us had begun to suffer the physical, emotional and mental side-effects of starvation. A few of the women had stopped getting their periods. Some of us had gotten weird rashes, or began losing hair. Drew had battled a bad case of diarrhea, which had left him weak and dehydrated until it stopped. I'd suffered from constipation, depression, social withdrawal and insomnia. I don't know if they were directly related to my lack of food, since the symptoms had first manifested themselves with the divorce. All of us were more irritable, and if the events of the last few hours were any indication, the others were now transitioning from irritability to full-blown psychotic episodes. I'd have to choose my words carefully when I confronted Chuck. I didn't want to challenge his Alpha Male status. Obviously, it was something that was important to him. I couldn't be perceived as a threat. But more importantly, I needed to appear reasonable and logical. I needed to persuade him that I no longer needed to die. Indeed, I'd killed so that the rest of them wouldn't have to. They didn't need to worry about it. The blood was on my hands, and from it, the others would stay alive a little while longer.

The lights buzzed overhead, the sound faint and ghostly. I clutched my spear tighter. Something moaned behind me. I spun around and gasped, my eyes widening. Clyde stumbled into the corridor, supporting himself with one hand against the wall. His other arm hung limp at his side. He was hunched over, but he lifted his head and stared at me with half-lidded eyes. The blood on his face made his skin seem stark and pale and ghostly. When he opened his mouth to speak, his teeth were bright red.

"I thought I killed you," I said. My voice seemed to echo down the hall.

"Uck oo, Eet…oer ucker…"

"I can't understand you, Clyde."

"Uck oo!" Clyde raised his hand and gave me the finger, relying on universal sign language to communicate for him.

"Listen…" I laid the spear down on the floor and held up my hands. "We don't have to do this, Clyde. You're hurt. You're hurt real bad. Let me go get you some help. You don't have to kill me. If you guys are determined to resort to cannibalism, then I won't stand in your way. But it doesn't have to be me that you eat. We can start with Krantz, Jim and George. Okay?"

Clyde drooled blood.

"Okay?" I asked again.

"Uck oo!"

"Fuck me? No, fuck you, Clyde. You've got two choices. You can sit down right here and let me get you some help, or I can finish the fucking job and make sure you're the first course at dinner tonight. Now, which do you prefer?"

He stared at me, his mouth hanging open, his wounded, bloody tongue lolling from between his lips like a dead fish. He swayed back and forth, and then slumped to the floor with a sigh. It was a slow, laborious process, and he grunted with pain as he pushed his back against the wall. His eyes never left me. They seemed accusatory, angry and distrustful.

"Good," I said, softening my voice. "That's good. Now you just stay right there, Clyde. I'll go work everything out with Chuck and get you some help. Stay calm and don't move. Just rest. I'll be back. Okay?"

He didn't respond, and I wondered if he understood me at all. A string of bloody drool dribbled down his chin. Then Clyde nodded slowly, and I saw a cautious hope in his gaze. The tension seemed to go out of his body. He closed his eyes. His head and shoulders sagged, and his chin drooped against his chest. I stood there for a moment, watching him, making sure that he wouldn't get back up and claw his way after me after I'd turned my back on him, but he didn't move. Were it not for the slow rise and fall of his chest, or the occasional twitch of his legs and feet, I'd have thought he was dead. I resisted the urge to prod him with my shoe. In truth, seeing him like that, I felt sorry for Clyde. I didn't feel guilt. At that point, I was beyond guilt. Maybe I was in shock. Maybe it was a mental defense mechanism—my psyche's way of shielding me from the crushing totality that I'd murdered three people and injured a fourth. Yes, it had been in self-defense, but at that moment, the facts didn't matter. Maybe you can't understand that. Maybe you have to have killed someone to sympathize with how I felt. I pitied Clyde, but I was also secure in the certainty that he'd brought it on himself.

After arming myself with the spear again, I started back down the corridor, passing by the restroom and heading toward the power plant. The roar of the generators grew louder and I could feel the floor vibrating slightly beneath my feet as I drew closer to the power plant. I turned around once, just to make sure Clyde was still there. He was. Then I focused my attention in front of me. A sign on the power plant door warned me of electrical hazards. That made me grin. Getting electrocuted seemed to be the least of my problems right now. Taking a deep breath, I pushed the door open and stepped inside.

The noise immediately quadrupled in volume. To say it was loud inside the power plant was an understatement. Loud didn't begin to describe it. Deafening was much more apt. It was the kind of noise you felt in your chest. I was used to it, of course. I had to experience it every time I'd given a tour. Still, after a few moments, my ears began to throb. If there was anyone inside the area, I'd never hear them, but on a more positive note, they wouldn't hear me either. The room was huge, taking up most of the bunker's upper level, and there were plenty of places for me to hide. In addition to the generators, the power plant held our massive fresh water tank and the center of the air filtration system. There was all sorts of other equipment, too. I was clueless to their origin or purpose, even as a tour guide and employee of the hotel. I'd never been mechanically inclined, and we'd never had to talk about them during the tour. But I didn't need to know what they were to hide behind or beneath them. There were plenty of dark corners and catwalks and areas filled with pipes and conduit and wires. Between that and the noise, I could have hid in the power plant indefinitely. It occurred to me then that the power plant should have been my first choice. Maybe if I'd gone there instead of to the blast door, Jim and George would still be alive.

Despite the extremity of the power plant, I took my time, proceeding cautiously. If I encountered someone inside here, I'd have a hard time reasoning with them if they couldn't hear me. It would be better to confront my pursuers outside of the area. I passed by a large, wheeled toolbox, the kind you usually saw in an automotive garage. It had belonged to one of our maintenance men. I paused for a moment, considering raiding it for more weapons. I experimented with the drawers and discovered that the toolbox wasn't locked. I rooted through it. It was full of everything you'd expect—wrenches, screwdrivers, hammers, gauges, shop rags, pneumatic and compressed air parts, and various mechanical odds and ends. I found a cigarette lighter and half a pack of matches. I grabbed both and stuffed them in my pocket. I also took a flat-end screwdriver and a box-cutter. I pushed the button on the box-cutter and the razor slid out of the end. The blade was rusty, but sharp. I pushed the button back down and stuck both the razor knife and the screwdriver in my back pocket. I considered taking one of the claw hammers but then decided to keep my spear instead. It would give me more reach should I need it. I hoped that I no longer would.

There were other potentially useful items scattered throughout the power plant. I opened a locker and found cans of gasoline, kerosene, and industrial solvents. Fire extinguishers and emergency eye-wash stations hung on the walls. A grease gun dangled from a length of angle iron. A long, black hose lay coiled on a skid. There were mops and whisk brooms in a corner, along with a wheeled mop bucket. There was also a portable sump pump, a wet-vac, and other pieces of equipment. I made a note of their location, and then continued on my way.

At the far end of the power plant was a stairwell that led back down to the bunker's lower level. I stood at the door for a moment, gathering my resolve. It would be futile to try to listen for someone on the other side, so I simply pushed the door open and stepped back, in case there was somebody waiting. There wasn't, so I stepped out into the stairwell. The thick door slammed shut behind me, immediately muffling the monotonous, numbing thrum of the generators. I looked out over the metal handrail and glanced below. The overhead lights were almost burned out, reduced to a single working bulb, but despite the shadows, I could see that the stairwell was empty. There was a landing halfway down, followed by another set of stairs with a door at the bottom. Nodding to myself, I started down. My arms and legs felt shaky—whether from hunger or nervousness, or maybe both. I reached the landing without incident and was just about to go down the second set of stairs when the door at the bottom opened. I retreated a few steps, my heart rate instantly pounding, and flattened myself against the wall. I realized at that moment that I was screwed. If I made a break for it, whoever was coming up the stairs would see me running and know where I'd gone. I had no choice but to confront them, and hope that they'd listen to reason.

Footsteps padded up the concrete stairs, echoing off the walls. The generators rumbled above me. Then a figure emerged onto the landing. I leaped forward and thrust my spear at them.

"Hold it!"

The figure cried out, startled. I recognized the voice. Then he stepped into the light.

"Pete? Jesus fucking Christ…"

"Drew?" I lowered my voice to a whisper. "What the hell are you doing?"

"Looking for you." He glanced down at my spear. The point was only inches from his stomach. "You planning on sticking me with that thing?"

"Sorry." I lowered my weapon. "I thought they'd killed you."

"No. Chuck was really pissed, but he let me go after I told them I'd help look for you. I was just coming to do that now. Here." He held up a bottle of water and offered it to me. "I thought you might be able to use that."

Nodding eagerly, I took the bottle from him. It was still cold and the plastic was covered with condensation. It felt wonderful. I rubbed it against my sweaty forehead and then unscrewed the cap and drank greedily, gulping it down. Water dribbled down my chin. I drank it all and then sighed.

"Thanks. I needed that."

"You're welcome. Are you okay?"

I nodded.

"So where have you been?" Drew asked. "They went ape-shit when they figured out you'd escaped the incinerator room. Chuck sent Jim, George and Clyde up here to look for you, along with the Chinese guy."

The Chinese guy—we called him that because none of us knew his name. He didn't speak a word of English and none of us spoke Chinese. His communication with our group had been accomplished through a series of hand gestures and grunts. He was nice enough. Middle-aged, slightly overweight (at least, when we first came here), but with a full, thick head of hair. He hadn't bothered anybody and nobody bothered him. I'd often wondered how he ended up at The Pocahontas. Had he been a guest? Had he been there with anybody else, and if so, how come they hadn't made it down to the bunker with him? Were they among the zombies now, or had he come alone?

"I didn't run into the Chinese guy," I said.

"He came back down a little bit ago," Drew explained. "To be honest, I don't think he completely understands what's going on. I mean, he voted and everything, but who knows if he understood what we were voting on. Chuck sent him up here with the others but then he came back down again, looking confused. He kept saying 'Dui bu chi' or something like that. Whatever that means. That's when Chuck sent me up here instead."

I grinned. "Good for Chinese dude. If we ever get out of here, I'll have to remember to buy him a beer. Where are the others?"

"Waiting downstairs." Drew glanced over his shoulder at the door, and then turned back to me. "Did you see Jim and the others?"

I nodded.

"What happened?"

"They're dead. Well, Jim and George are dead. Clyde's still alive, but he's hurt. I fucked him up pretty bad, I think."

"You killed them?"

"I had to. They would have killed me if I hadn't."

Drew nodded slowly. "Yeah, they would have. Jesus, what's become of us, Pete? This whole kill or be killed thing really sucks."

"Yes, it does. But I don't see that we have an option, Drew."

"No, I guess we don't."

"I was thinking about trying to reason with Chuck. Make some kind of deal. With Jim, George and Krantz all dead, it's not like they have to eat me anymore. If they're so set on eating each other, they can start with them."

"Do you think Chuck and the others will agree to that?"

I shrugged. "I don't know. You saw them last. What was their temperature like?"

"Chuck's pretty damned livid. He's never been your biggest fan to begin with. This hasn't helped."

"We got off on the wrong foot. Maybe he just needs to get to know me better."

It took Drew a moment to realize that I was making a joke. When he did, a slight smile crossed his face. He seemed uneasy and nervous. I chided myself for being so inconsiderate. Here was my one friend, the one person I could count on not to stick me in the back, and I was making him stand out here in the open while the hunt was still in progress.

"So," Drew asked finally. "What now?"

I shrugged again. "I guess I go and face the music. If they won't listen to reason, then we've got a fight on our hands. But I don't want to endanger you any more than I already have. You should stay here. I'll confront Chuck by myself."

"No, I'll go with you. He's in the lunch room, with most of the others. If you go by yourself, there's a chance someone might see you and attack first and then ask questions later. If I'm with you, I might be able to get them to hold off."

"I can't ask you to do that, Drew."

"You didn't ask me to. I volunteered. Besides, I told Chuck I'd look for you. This way, I can show him that I did as he asked. Might buy me some slack with him."

"Okay," I agreed, albeit somewhat reluctantly. I don't know. Maybe it was my conscience trying to counterbalance the murders I'd just committed, but at that moment, I was more scared of Drew paying the consequences for my actions than I was of losing my own life. Drew was a good guy. He was my friend—the only real friend I had down here in the bunker. Allowing Chuck and the others to punish him for something I'd done would be a form of betrayal, and I couldn't do that to him. Not after everything that had happened.

We started down the stairs. When we reached the door on the lower level, Drew paused, eyeing my spear.

"I'd feel a lot better if I had a weapon, too."

"Here." I pulled the screwdriver out of my back pocket and handed it to him. "Use this. It ain't much, but if you stab somebody, it should do the job. Hopefully, it won't come to that."

"Let's hope so."

I put my ear to the door and listened. It was quiet. Drew had said that Chuck and most of the others were in the lunchroom. Given the silence on the other side of the door, there was a good chance that the hallway was currently unoccupied. If my luck held out, maybe we could make it to the lunchroom without an altercation. If I approached Chuck with deference and respect, maybe this whole thing could be turned around before it went any further.

"So are we going, or what?" Drew whispered.

Nodding, I opened the door.

Chuck and five others were waiting on the other side. With him were the Chinese guy, Emma Straub, Mike Blazi, Jeff Antonio, and Dave Lombardo. I've already told you about the Chinese guy. Emma was a young woman who had worked upstairs in the hotel's candy shop. She'd been very pretty before starvation had begun ravaging her face and body. Mike, Jeff and Dave were documentary filmmakers who had been staying at the Pocahontas and playing lots of golf, until the zombies showed up and ruined their game. None of them were armed but there was murder in their eyes.

Chuck grinned. "Hi, Pete. Welcome! So glad you could join us."

"Shit."

I let go of the door. It started to swing shut, but Dave reached out and grabbed it with one hand. I backed up, not wanting to turn my back on them, and felt the flat, hard edge of Drew's screwdriver press into my shirt, right above my kidney. I stiffened.

"Sorry, Pete," he said. "I'm really sorry. Just don't move, okay?"

"Drew, what the hell is going on?"

"They were going to kill me if I didn't help find you. I'm

sorry, dude. I really am. But I didn't survive those walking fucking corpses just to end up being killed down here."

"You stupid motherfucker…"

"Enough of that," Chuck said. "Good job, Drew. Now do me a favor? Run upstairs and tell those other worthless ass-clowns to get back down here."

"I can't."

"Why not?"

"Because they're dead," Drew told him. "And before you do anything to Pete, I think we ought to hear him out."

Dave and Chuck stepped toward me. I tried to move away, but all that did was drive the screwdriver harder against my back. Any more pressure and the tip would break my skin.

"It's true," I said. "George and Jim are dead, and Clyde is hurt pretty bad. I left him upstairs. He needs medical attention."

"So," Chuck said, "in addition to Krantz, you've murdered two more of my people."

"They're not *your* people, Chuck. They're just people—survivors, trying to stay alive. Yes, I killed them, but it was in self-defense, and it was no different than what you plan to do to me."

"We're doing what we have to," Emma said. "To survive."

"Well, now you don't have to. Don't you guys see? Krantz, Jim and George—that's enough to feed all of you for months, if you prepare their bodies now, before they start to rot. You don't have to kill me. You don't have to kill anyone! I've done all the hard work for you. There's no reason this has to go on a minute longer. Let's just all calm down and take a deep breath, okay?"

Behind me, I felt the pressure from the screwdriver tip ease a little. Drew's breath tickled the back of my neck.

"I'm sorry," he whispered.

I ignored him.

The Chinese guy looked at each of us, trying to figure out what was going on. Emma, Jeff and Mike paused, seemingly surprised by this revelation. They glanced at each other, and then at Chuck, who appeared nonplussed. He was still grinning. Dave was not. Dave stared straight into my eyes, unblinking. I glanced down and noticed with some unease that he had a bulge in the front of his pants. Dave liked what was happening, and that made him my first target, should things not play out the way I'd hoped them to.

Chuck turned to Jeff and Mike. "Go upstairs and get Jim and George's bodies. Put them with Krantz.

They nodded, and then stepped toward me. Drew backed up so that I could move aside, and in doing so, removed the screwdriver from my back. Dave had to step aside, as well, so that Jeff and Mike could slip past us and up the stairs. Mike couldn't meet my eyes, but Jeff did.

"It was nothing personal," he told me. "I hope you understand that."

I shrugged. "The bodies are down near the blast door, where the forklifts are parked. That's where you'll find Clyde, too."

"Okay."

They started up the stairs, leaving me at the bottom of the stairwell with Drew, Chuck, Dave, Emma and the Chinese guy. Emma and the Chinese guy were still in the hallway. The others were crowded around me, close enough that I could smell their stink. Above us, the echoes of Mike and Jeff's footsteps quickly faded. I heard the door open and close as they entered the power plant.

Chuck's grin returned. "Dave, take Pete's weapon, will you?"

Flinching, I tightened my grip on the spear. "Are we cool now, Chuck?"

"Oh, we're very cool. You've done us the favor of providing food for the group. I'll repay the favor with a quick death."

Dave and Chuck lunged at me simultaneously. Dave grabbed the spear and tried to rip it from my hands, but I held on tight. Behind me, I heard Drew cry out in surprise. Without looking, I stomped hard on his foot. He yelped, and I heard the screwdriver clatter to the floor. Chuck grabbed a fistful of my hair and yanked hard as I kneed Dave in the balls. The big man grunted, and the air whooshed from his lungs and into my face. It reeked. He stumbled backward, cradling his groin, and slammed into the wall. The door slammed shut, blocking Emma and the Chinese guy from view. I hollered as Chuck pulled my hair. He twisted, trying to force my head down.

"Let go of me, motherfucker."

"This is my bunker," Chuck spat. "My people. *My fucking people!* You don't question me and get away with it, Pete. You made me look bad."

I realized then that for Chuck, this wasn't about survival. It wasn't about starving to death. It was about power. With a scream, I jerked away from him. A fistful of my hair ripped free. I thrust my spear blindly, jabbing Chuck in the side. Dave moaned on the floor. Chuck yelled something unintelligible. I spun around and with my right palm, I slammed Drew's head against the wall. Then I ran back up the stairs.

"Get him!" Chuck's enraged cry boomed, echoing in the stairwell.

I heard footsteps pursuing me, but rather than turn around to see who it was, I ran faster, scrambling up the stairs two at a time. My scalp felt hot, and I was pretty sure I was bleeding, but I didn't care. I rounded the corner and fled up the second flight of stairs. I half expected the door to the power plant to burst open as Jeff and Mike returned to investigate the commotion, but then I remembered that they wouldn't be able to hear us over the generators.

Fingers grasped at my shirttail, pulling me backward. I swung the spear like a club, lashing out at whoever was behind me. The spear whistled through the air and then I connected with my pursuer's head with a loud, solid whack. They grunted, and slipped. I heard them scrabbling on the stairs, along with Chuck's cursing and commands and Dave's moans. I reached the door, yanked it open, and bolted into the power plant. There was no immediate sign of Jeff and Mike. The door slammed shut behind me, then banged open again a split second later as Drew charged into the room. I turned and faced him. He was panting hard and his face was red. His eyes widened and he held up his hands.

"Pete, listen to me…"

I charged him, my face twisted with rage. Drew's eyes got even wider. Then he turned around and fled. My spear thrust clanged uselessly against the closing door.

My first instinct was to chase him, but instead, I shoved my spear through the door handle so that they couldn't open it from that end. Then, keeping an eye out for Jeff and Mike, I raced over to one of the work stations I'd spotted earlier. I grabbed a can of gasoline, twisted off the cap and poured the contents into the mop bucket. Then I stuffed an oily shop rag in my pocket and wheeled the bucket over to the door. Using my lighter, I lit the rag on fire. Then, as it slowly burned, I pulled the spear free and opened the door.

Chuck, Drew and Dave were halfway up the second landing. Drew and Dave were side-by-side. Chuck was just behind them. He wasn't smiling anymore. Drew's face was flushed, and his lip was swollen and bleeding. Apparently, Dave or Chuck had convinced him to turn around again. They faltered when they saw me with the burning rag. I held it out, letting it dangle in the air. The flames climbed higher, singeing the hair on my knuckles and hand. I didn't care. In truth, I barely felt it.

Without a word, I nudged the bucket forward with my foot and sent it rolling toward the stairs. I dropped the flaming shop rag into it and jumped back. The effect was instantaneous. There was a loud 'whoom' and a bright flare as the gasoline caught on fire.

"Shit," Dave yelled. "Get the fuck back!"

His warning came too late. The mop bucket reached the top stair and tilted over with a loud crash, spilling flaming gasoline toward them. Fire raced down the stairs, licking Drew and Dave's feet and flowing toward Chuck. He jumped to the bottom of the landing, rolled, and fled down the next flight of stairs. Drew and Dave tried running, too, but they couldn't outrun the fire creeping up their legs. Both men screamed. Drew tripped and fell, pulling Dave down with him. Their shrieks grew louder as the flames engulfed them. The stairwell filled with smoke and the stench of burning flesh. Their hair caught fire next. Despite everything, my stomach grumbled. I closed my eyes to block out the horrible sight, and the smell changed. The stench of burning human flesh became the aroma of roasting pork. I thought back to the day that Alyssa and I got married. The caterer provided an open pit pig roast for our wedding reception, which was held outdoors. All of the guests had agreed that it was a great meal. Whenever anybody talked about that day, the first thing they invariably mentioned was how good the food had been. Alyssa's father had eaten three servings of roasted pork, and would have eaten more if the disc jockey hadn't called him front and center to dance with Alyssa to "Daddy's Little Girl".

Drew and Dave were both fully engulfed in flames now. They rolled down the stairs, shrieking and beating at themselves. The smoke made my eyes water.

The smell made my mouth water.

The fire alarm began to wail. A second later, the bunker's automatic sprinkler system kicked on, showering the stairwell with water. Drew and Dave popped and sizzled. I stood there at the top of the stairs, stretched out my arms and tilted my head upward, letting the spray wash over me. I opened my mouth and drank greedily. I groaned in pleasure as the water ran down my head and chest and back. It felt like a baptism. I wondered what Eisenhower's bronze head would have thought of me, had it been able to see me at that moment. Would it have been proud? And what about Alyssa? If she could have seen me at that moment, would she have seen me for the man I really was? Would *she* have been proud? Would she have regretted her decision?

I decided that I really didn't care anymore.

"Fuck her and fuck them. Fuck them all."

I was tired of being the prey. It was time to become the hunter. Nodding in satisfaction, I ducked back into the power plant and made preparations for war.

SIX

The bunker's sprinkler system was fairly advanced. Only the sprinklers in the stairwell were activated. The alarm bleated for several minutes, though. The shrill wail was audible even over the generators. I knew that Jeff and Mike would hear it, so I hid behind one of the tanks and waited for them to arrive.

I didn't have to wait long. Jeff came hurrying along at a trot a few minutes later, looking bewildered. There was no sign of Mike. I wondered if perhaps they had already reached the bodies, and decided that Mike should stay with Clyde while Jeff investigated the source of the alarm.

In his hurry, he didn't see me hiding behind the tank. I waited until he'd gone past me. Then I slipped out from behind the tank and sneaked up behind him. I didn't have to worry about him hearing me. Between the fire alarm and the generators, there was no chance of that. The extreme heat in the power plant had already dried most of the water the sprinkler system had sprayed me with, so I also wasn't worried about him seeing puddles.

Despite my caution, Jeff paused. He raised his head slightly and sniffed the air. His back was still turned to me. I assumed he'd noticed the smell coming from the stairwell. Before he could move again, I pulled the box-cutter from my pocket, extended the blade, and rushed up behind him. I looped my arm around his forehead and slashed at his throat with my other hand.

Cutting someone's throat isn't at all like it appears in the movies. When you see Rambo or Michael Myers slit somebody's throat, it's always quick and easy and arterial blood immediately starts spraying from the victim's wound. It wasn't like that at all with Jeff. I don't know if I cut too low or too high, or not deep enough, but there was no crimson

77

geyser. He screamed, more from surprise than pain, I think, and tried to pull away. I was surprised that he was still able to make noise. He slipped my hold on him, got free and spun around. There was a thin, red line on his neck, almost like the indentation from a necklace chain that had been worn too long. I don't think he was even aware of it at first, but then the pain must have kicked in. He reached up slowly and touched the wound with his fingertips, probing it gently, experimentally. When he pushed on it, a few red drops leaked out. Jeff pulled his hand away and looked at his fingertips. More blood began to flow, but it was nowhere near what I'd imagined.

"You cut me."

I couldn't hear him, but I understood him just the same. I leaped at him, slashing with the box-cutter. The razor sliced him just below the shoulder. When he reflexively reached toward the wound, I swiped the blade across the back of his hand. Jeff tried to turn and run, but I jumped on him, stabbing again and again with the box-cutter. He thrashed and kicked beneath me, but I managed to stay on top of him. I just kept jamming the blade into his back and shoulders and neck and head. Sometimes, the razor got pushed back up into the sheath and I'd thumb it out again, even while I struck him with my other fist. We went on like that for a long time. I don't know how long, exactly. I know that his struggles weakened, and then ceased, and even after he'd stopped moving altogether, I kept on stabbing and slashing at him. It was exactly like what had happened with George, except that this time I had a knife. My hands, legs and face were splattered with blood, and my clothes were sticky and wet again.

When I stood up, blood dripped from my fingertips and the edge of the knife. I put the bloody weapon back in my pocket. Then I rolled Jeff over and searched him for anything useful. He had nothing on him except for his car keys and a black leather wallet. I ignored the keys and gave the wallet a cursory examination. It contained a few one, five and ten dollar bills, totally useless in the current environment, unless you were using them to start a fire or as toilet paper. In one of the wallet's pockets, there was also a round wooden token with the slogan *IT IS WHAT IT IS* emblazoned on it. That made me grin.

"It is what it is," I muttered. "Do whatever you have to do to survive, and if the situation changes, adapt or die."

The other side of the wooden coin had the name of what I presumed was a strip club—The Odessa, Lewisberry, PA. After a moment, I stuck the token in my front pocket. Then I rifled through the rest of the wallet. All that was left were some pictures of a woman and two kids. The children looked exactly like Jeff. I didn't linger on the pictures too long, because looking at them made me feel bad. I closed the wallet, but not before noticing that I'd left bloody thumbprint smudges all over Jeff's family's faces. I dropped the wallet on his corpse and stood up. When I walked away, the soles of my shoes stuck to the floor, and I left red footprints in my wake.

The fire alarm ceased wailing as abruptly as it had begun. The roar of the generators seemed almost subdued in its absence. There was no way of telling how long I had before Mike came looking for Jeff, or how soon Chuck and the others would recover from my attack and launch a new strike. I hurried over to the stairwell door and jammed my spear through the door handle. Not satisfied with that, I wheeled one of the heavy toolboxes over to the door, as well, and shoved the toolbox against it. Satisfied it would hold, I wiped my forehead with the back of my hand and sighed.

Moving the toolbox was hard work. It was heavy, and would have been difficult even if I wasn't weak with hunger. When I was finished, I had to resist the urge to sit down and rest. Instead, I rummaged through the toolbox until I found a pencil and a small, pocket-sized tablet. Then I returned to my hiding place behind the machinery and began making a list of everyone that had been inside the bunker when the siege had begun. I crossed off Annie, Ryan, Milo, Rachel and everyone else who had died before the decision to resort to democratic cannibalism had been decided upon. That left a population of seventeen, not counting myself. Seventeen people who had voted to eat me, except for Drew—and possibly the Chinese guy, who might not have understood what they were voting on. But while he might not have understood everything that was happening, he'd stood by Chuck and the others earlier. That made him an enemy. The same went for good old Drew, who had sold me out in the end like some cheap prison snitch.

I stuck the pencil in my mouth and chewed on the eraser, working up some saliva to ease my thirst as I pondered the situation.

Seventeen enemy combatants. I crossed off the ones I'd already killed—Krantz, George, Jim, Jeff, Dave and that back-stabbing son of a bitch Drew. True, Dave and Drew could have survived my attack, but if so, they were badly burned at the very least, and shouldn't be much trouble. With those six out of the way, that left Chuck, Mike, Clyde, Chinese Guy, Emma, Phillips, Nicole, Damonte, Susan, Ritchie, and Charles. I've already told you about half of them. Nicole Baez was twenty-five who did body-piercing at a tattoo studio in Lewisburg and had worked at the hotel on weekends. Ritchie Giffen and Damonte Williams had also been Pocahontas staff. Susan Fremont was a local who had been at the Pocahontas to arrange her daughter's wedding reception. Finally, there was Charles St. John Smith III, or Charles the Third as he'd insisted we call him several times. Charles was from Philadelphia, and worked in the music industry. He'd supposedly been, at various times, a disc jockey at WKDU 91.7, a promoter at punk clubs like House of Conflict and Stalag 13 (which I'd heard of even down here in West Virginia) and had played in a hardcore band. Charles had been passing through when the zombies attacked. He hadn't even been staying at the hotel. He'd been gassing up his car across the street and fled here when the shit kicked off. None of them were people I'd have expected to go along with Chuck's insane plan, but evidently, all of them had.

Ten enemies remained. Ten people that I had to kill in order to survive. Eleven if I counted Clyde. I had tried to reason with them, to negotiate mutually agreeable terms that we could abide by, but Chuck and his people wanted none of that. And they were Chuck's people. None of them had spoken up in protest when he called them that during our argument. The only conclusion I could draw from their behavior was that the others felt the same way Chuck did—and therefore, fuck them. I considered writing their names on my forearm, the same way Bruce Willis had done in the first *Die Hard* movie, but I couldn't because I didn't have a magic marker and the pencil wouldn't write on my skin. Pity, that. I would have enjoyed crossing their names out one by one in their own blood. I wished I had an iPod loaded with nothing but Motorhead songs. I'd have stalked the corridors of the bunker, slashing throats and smashing heads to the left and to the right, grinning a rictus grin and bathing in blood with "Orgasmatron" and "Killed By Death" on repeat providing the perfect soundtrack for slaughter. If I closed my eyes, I could picture it all. Even better, I could hear the music in all of its ear-splitting glory. I could smell the blood, feel its warmth as it sprayed across my skin. I could taste …

At that moment, I realized I'd been laughing, and the razor knife was back in my hands. I'd been fondling it. Worse, the crotch of my pants was stiff, and not just from the quickly-drying blood encrusting it. I had an erection, the first one I'd had in several weeks. Before, I'd thought that perhaps starvation was effecting that part of my body. Yes, I still got horny. I got horny all the time, especially when sitting in the movie room. But I'd been unable to muster much of a response in the past few weeks. Now I realized that it hadn't been that I lacked food or nutrition. The reason had been that I lacked the proper motivation and visual stimulation. Now I had them again, and my body responded in kind. I remembered that something similar had happened to Dave right before I'd had to kill him. Maybe Dave hadn't been such a bad guy, after all.

I became aware of a feint sound, nearly inaudible beneath the noise of the generators. It had a deliberate cadence, but no matter how hard I listened, I couldn't figure out what the sound was. A voice, possibly? If so, I'd find out who they were and where they were soon enough. It was time to go to work. My first step was to find Mike. After I'd taken care of him, I'd finish Clyde off. Then I'd take care of the others.

As I walked toward the exit, bloody box-cutter in hand, I heard that strange sound again. This time, I was definitely sure it was a voice, but it was still too faint and disjointed to figure out who was speaking. I tried humming to make it go away, but it remained, ethereal and persistent.

"Ready or not," I said, "here I come."

I opened the door and stepped boldly out into the hall, not caring if someone saw me or not. In truth, I wanted them to see me. I wanted them to be afraid. I wanted them to know that death was coming for them, not at the hands of some shambling, rotting corpse, but a living, breathing human being—a man who still possessed that spark we call a soul. A man whose soul they had collaborated to snuff out.

It turned out that I was indeed spotted almost immediately. Down at the far end of the corridor, Mike knelt over Clyde. When he saw me coming, he jumped up and ran toward me. I kept the same unhurried pace, as if I were just out for a leisurely Sunday afternoon stroll. The door swung shut behind me, once again muting the noise of the power plant.

When Mike had crossed about half the distance between us, he stopped short and stood there gaping at me. I must have made quite a horrific sight, covered in gore and grinning like a madman. Except that it wasn't gore. It was my new skin. And I definitely wasn't crazy. I've always believed that if you start out sane, you know when you cross over into insanity. That's the way it always works, right? When these people on the news finally snap and shoot up their office or their school or butcher their families and loved ones, they usually kill themselves afterward. That's because they know the enormity of what they've done. They know it was an act of insanity, and they can't bare to live with the consequences. That was how I knew I wasn't crazy. Not only could I live with the consequences of what I was doing—I was relishing them. It was the consequences of what I was doing that were keeping me alive. My only regret was that I hadn't figured that out earlier. Maybe then I wouldn't have wasted so much time feeling guilty over what I'd done to Krantz or the others.

Mike continued to stare at me. His expression was one of shocked disbelief. Then he turned around and fled down the hall.

I laughed. "That's no good, Mike. Where are you going to run to? The blast door is your only exit."

If he heard me, he gave no indication. He raced past Clyde without pause and clambered up onto the closest forklift. Still laughing, I continued walking toward him, purposely taking my time in order to draw things out. The laughter felt like ashes in my throat a moment later when Mike turned on one of the propane bottles and then started the forklift. Earlier, I hadn't thought to check if the keys were still in the ignitions. Obviously, Mike had. The engine choked and sputtered, and then roared to life.

"Hey," I shouted, stopping in my tracks. This wasn't what I had expected. "What the hell are you doing, Mike?"

Ignoring me, he fumbled with the shift. The gears grumbled and the hydraulics whined, and then Mike gave it gas, backing the forklift out of the cul-de-sac and whipping it around to face me. His expression—a strange, desperate mix of fear and determination—probably should have unnerved me, but it didn't. Instead, it just made me start laughing again.

"Okay, Mike. Is this the way you want it? Come on, then!"

I stuck the box-cutter in my back pocket and pulled off my bloody shirt. While I was pulling the shirt over my head, Mike floored it and the forklift shot toward me, racing past Clyde's still form. The hydraulics shrieked at a fevered pitch. The heavy steel forks banged and clanked. I ripped the shirt free and dangled it in front of me with both hands, waving it back and forth like a bullfighter in the ring.

"Come on, motherfucker. Toro! TORO!"

He gave it more gas and the forklift barreled down the corridor. I stood in the middle of the hallway, my feet spread shoulder-width apart and my knees locked, frantically urging him on with my makeshift matador cape. Mike shouted—a long, unintelligible cry of frustration and anger and fear. He hunched over the steering wheel, gripping it tight, and zeroed the forks in on me. I waited until the very last moment and then jumped aside. The forklift zipped past me. I grabbed one of the roll cage bars and pulled myself up onto the machine. I coughed, tasting exhaust fumes in the back of my throat.

Mike tried to push me off with one hand while he steered with the other, but I was ready for him. I slashed at the back of his hand with the box-cutter. The razor sliced deep, opening a long gash that ran from between the knuckles of his middle and ring fingers all the way down to his wrist. Shrieking, Mike yanked his hand away, but I slashed again, cutting his wrist and forearm. I expected him to punch me or try pushing me off again, or maybe crash us into the wall, but instead of doing that, Mike dove off the other side of the forklift and rolled across the floor. Immediately, the forklift began to lose speed and waver out of control, heading for the wall. The engine stuttered. I quickly slid into the driver's seat and took control of the wheel. Then I turned around. My arc was too wide and the forks scraped against the wall, gouging into the concrete.

I'd expected to see Mike fleeing down the corridor again, but instead, he lay on the floor, half-curled into the fetal position, and cradling his right ankle. His lips were drawn back in an anguished sneer, exposing nicotine-stained teeth, and his eyes were squeezed shut. Tears ran down his face.

"Did you break your ankle, Mike?" I shouted over the engine. "Gee, that's a tough break."

I maneuvered toward him.

"Get it, Mike? I said that's a tough break."

Moaning, he tried to stand up. His injured ankle buckled beneath him and he fell down again. His whimpers turned to screams as he began to crawl away, dragging his leg behind him.

I shook my head. "Some people just don't have a sense of humor."

Mike screamed in response.

I took my foot off the brake and eased the forklift forward. Then I stomped the accelerator. The forks and chassis blocked my view of Mike, but my aim was true. The fat tires crunched up and over his body, silencing his cries. The entire forklift bounced and jostled, as if I'd hit a particularly large pothole. Then it smoothed out again. I glanced behind me and smiled with approval. His head and pelvis had both been crushed, leaving behind a flattened, twisted thing and crimson tire tracks.

I heard the voice again. This time it was louder. Clearer. It sounded just like Alyssa, but that couldn't be.

"Pete, they're coming..."

"Alyssa?"

There was no response. I turned around and faced forward in my seat, intent on parking the forklift back in the cul-de-sac. Instead, I jerked in surprise when I saw Ritchie coming out of the shower room. He and the others hadn't been able to break my blockade in the power plant, so while I'd been busy taking care of Mike, Ritchie had shimmied up the incinerator chute, just as I'd done earlier.

Ritchie's eyes widened when he saw me. He glanced at Clyde, still sitting slumped over with his back against the wall, and then he turned back to me and Mike. For a moment, I thought he might charge me, and perhaps try to jump up into the cab the same way I'd done with Mike. He must have panicked, however, because instead of doing that or retreating to the restrooms, he darted the rest of the way out into the hall and ran towards the blast door. I stomped the accelerator and sped after him. As I passed by the shower room, I saw a second figure fleeing into the restroom. The door swung shut before I could determine who it was.

Ritchie reached the blast door, looked over his shoulder at me, and then shouted something. I couldn't hear him over the forklift's engine, but I could still hear Alyssa. She was urging me on. Then Ritchie did something completely unexpected— he grabbed the wheel that opened the blast door.

"Oh, shit."

Weakened by hunger, Ritchie strained to turn the wheel.

"Ritchie," I shouted, "what the hell are you doing? You'll let them in!"

Nodding, he strained harder. His limbs shook from the exertion, but despite his efforts, the door didn't budge. Ritchie shot a hurried, panicked glance back at me, and then wiped his hands on his pants and tried again.

I hurriedly worked the controls. The forks could be tilted up and down and side to side, so that they'd fit under different sized skids. They were also tapered so that they were narrower near the front. I raised them, drawing the forks close together so that there was no gap between them, forming a giant spear of sorts. Gunning the engine, I aimed them at Ritchie. Instead of running, he redoubled his efforts. He was still trying to turn the wheel when I rammed into him. The forks punched through his chest and hit the steel blast door behind him. The noise was incredible. It was like standing inside a bell tower. My ears rang. The force of the impact threw me from the seat, slamming me against the wire mesh of the roll cage. My mouth filled with blood. I relished the taste.

The crash stalled the forklift. I fumbled with the controls again, trying to restart the engine so that I could raise the forks higher, but the forklift wouldn't start. Ritchie was still alive, but just barely. As I watched, he reached behind him, clawing at the forks with his bloody hands. He couldn't quite reach them. I climbed down from the cab as his head drooped onto his chest. I felt for a pulse and found none.

"Are you dead?"

I slapped his head and then flicked his ear with my thumb and middle finger. Ritchie didn't respond.

"Yeah," I said. "I guess you are. What the hell were you thinking? We can't open the door. If we could, none of this would be happening."

I hurried over to Clyde and knelt beside his still form. Then I put my fingers to his throat and checked his pulse, as well. I couldn't find one, and his skin was cool to the touch. He'd bled out, dying while I was occupied with the others. Humming the bass line from Queen's 'Another One Bites the Dust', I stood up and strolled toward the restroom. I began to sing aloud. My voice echoed off the walls. Giggling, I spun around and did a quick moonwalk. Then I knocked on the bathroom door.

"Housekeeping. I'm here to scrub the toilet. Anybody home?"

I pushed the door open and stepped inside. The bathroom was empty. I got down on my hands and knees and peered under the stall. I saw no feet but there was a shadow on the floor around the toilet. As I watched, the shadow moved. Grinning, I stood up again.

"Hello?"

I waited for a few seconds more and then I made a big show of walking towards the door. I stepped hard so that my footfalls would be heard. I opened the door and let it slam close. Then I stood still and waited.

Inside the stall, someone whimpered. I held my breath, resisting the urge to charge. I heard sounds of movement. Slowly, the stall door opened. The Chinese guy walked out, saw me, and screamed.

"Howdy." I winked at him.

"Duì bù qǐ," he cried. "Duì bù qǐ. Duì bù qǐ…"

"I don't understand what you're saying."

He flung his hands up in front of his face and cringed. "Bù, bùyào shā wǒ. Du ìb ùqǐ!"

I took a tentative step toward him. The Chinese guy began to weep. A dark stain appeared on the front of his pants and the restroom filled with the sharp stench of piss.

"Dude, you could have at least used the urinal!"

"Bù, bùyào shā wǒ," he wept. "Duì bù qǐ. Bù, bùyào shā wǒ…"

My head began to hurt. His sobs were like knives stabbing into my brain. My temples throbbed. The pain made it hard to hear Alyssa. I strode across the floor. The Chinese guy tried to run past me, but I grabbed his arm and swung him around. He crashed into the mirror over the sink, shattering the glass. Jagged shards clattered off the porcelain and onto the floor. Before he could recover, I twisted his arm behind him and shoved him against the wall. With my other hand, I reached up and grabbed a fistful of his hair. Twisting it in my fist, I slammed his face into the broken mirror. The Chinese guy shrieked.

"Nǐ húndàn!"

"Shut up."

His screams turned guttural and frantic.

"Shut up." I slammed his face into the glass again and again, punctuating each blow with another command. "Shut up. Shut up. Shut up."

I spun him away from the mirror and threw him to the

floor. Silver fragments jutted from his forehead and cheeks, and his lips were swollen and bleeding. Groaning, he tried to roll away, but I kicked him in the side of the head. He started to cry out again, but I stepped on his throat. His eyes bulged and his mouth hung open. I stared down at him, impassive.

"You brought this on yourself. You may not speak the language, but you knew what the hell was going on."

I put all my weight—what little of it was left after weeks with no food—on his throat, and stood there until he was dead. Slowly, I became aware of a loud breathing in the restroom with me. I listened to the panting sound, and then realized that it was me. I stared at the broken mirror. A few cracked shards dangled in the upper left corner and I could see my reflection in them. I felt a momentary surge of shock. It was quite a sight. I was a mess.

"Pete…"

"Alyssa?" I glanced around the restroom, but it was empty. "Where are you?"

"I'm here. I'm right here."

"Where?"

"Come find me, Pete. Catch me if you can…"

"Alyssa!"

The restroom began to spin. It was hard to breathe. My chest, limbs and head felt heavy. There was a rushing sound in my ears, as if a wall of water was bearing down on me. Dark spots floated in front of my eyes, and suddenly, it was unbearably hot. Sweat poured down my face. My hands and feet tingled. Then the rushing sound changed into a constant, steady ringing. I felt extremely weak and sleepy. The ringing grew louder.

"Aly—"

And then the hunger and weakness and exertion and shock caught up with me, and I collapsed on top of the Chinese guy. The last thing I was aware of was the smell of his blood.

SEVEN

When I woke up, I wasn't sure where I was at first. The last thing I remembered was calling out for Alyssa. With my eyes still shut, I rolled over and wondered where she was. Something wet squelched beneath me. I opened my eyes and found myself face to face with the Chinese guy. I was laying on top of him. His body was cold, and so was I. Shuddering, I jumped up and off of him, and skittered across the floor till my back was against the urinal. I stared around in confusion, until it all started to come back to me.

I sat there shivering as my full consciousness slowly returned. The Chinese guy was dead. I felt no qualms or guilt about it. The only thing I felt at all was tired. Oh, I had a vague sense of satisfaction, but there were seven more people to kill yet, and I wasn't sure that I had the strength to continue—not without a nap first. That was out of the question, though. Passing out had been bad enough. Any one of my remaining enemies—Chuck, Emma, Phillips, Nicole, Damonte, Susan, or Charles—could have snuck into the restroom while I was unconscious and that would have been it for me. In truth, I was surprised that they hadn't. Could they be waiting outside the door, perhaps? Or maybe Ritchie and the Chinese guy had been the only ones able to climb up the incinerator chute?

With some difficulty, I stripped the Chinese guy's shirt off and put it on so that I wasn't running around half-naked anymore. Then, I slowly clambered to my feet. My legs were still a bit wobbly and when I stood up all the way, the room began to spin again. I closed my eyes and took several deep breaths. My head was still throbbing, and I wondered if I'd bumped it when I passed out. I felt my scalp, but there were no new cuts or lumps. The ringing in my ears had subsided. The restroom was quiet. After a few more deep breaths, I opened my eyes again, and was relieved to discover that the dizziness had passed. I stepped over Chinese guy's corpse and stood in front of the sink. I avoided looking at my reflection in the broken mirror. Instead, I turned on the spigot and cupped my hands beneath it. The cold water felt luxuriant. I splashed my face and head several times. Then I scrubbed the blood and grime away, and dried off with paper towels from the dispenser. When I was finished, I felt alert and awake and reinvigorated.

I opened the restroom door, walked out into the hall and got hit in the face by something long and hard.

Then I passed out again.

***

This time, I came to with a start, fully remembering everything that had happened before. The pain in my head was worse now, and my mouth was pure agony. I moaned, sick to my stomach from the pain. Every time I breathed through my mouth, the air passing over my split lips made me wince. I tried breathing through my nose and found that doing so hurt even worse than breathing through my mouth. My nostrils felt like they'd been stuffed with wet cotton. I tried moving my jaw to alleviate the pressure in my nose and ears, but all that brought was tears to my eyes and more pain. I didn't think my nose was broken, but it was definitely fucked up.

"I don't think it's broken," a male voice said. "Looks sort of like a sliced plum, if you want to know the truth. I think the nail sticking out of that board caught you dead center."

I opened my eyes and saw Charles St. John Smith III—he of the long name—staring at me. His expression was placid. Almost serene.

"Hi, Pete. You really lost your shit, didn't you?"

I parted my mouth to speak and immediately regretted it. A fresh jolt of agony wracked my body. I choked back a scream and squeezed my eyes shut again. When I tried to move my arms, I found that I couldn't. I prodded my teeth with my tongue and discovered that several of them had been broken. My nausea grew worse. I opened my eyes again and studied my surroundings. I was lying on the floor in the main corridor. Clyde lay across from me. My arms had been bound flat against my sides with black electrical wiring. The covering must have been worn off in some places, because I felt the copper digging into my skin.

Charles was crouched on his haunches in front of me. In one hand, he clutched a length of wood from a skid. A bent nail jutted from one end. My skin and blood decorated the tip of the nail. At five feet, eight inches tall, Charles was anything but an imposing figure. When we'd first sought refuge inside the bunker, the thirty-two year old had weighed about one hundred and forty-five pounds. Now he weighed considerably less. Still, that hadn't prevented him from knocking me on my ass and tying me up. I flexed my arms, testing the bonds. They held firm. I opened my mouth slightly and spoke in halting, clipped tones.

"Where's…Chuck…?"

"Downstairs." Charles nodded his head toward the power plant. "All of them are downstairs. Me, Ritchie and that Chinese guy were the only ones who could climb up the incinerator chute. Damonte and Phillips are both too big, still. I think they've been hoarding food. How about you? Do you think they've got a secret stash somewhere?"

I tried to shrug, but the wires prevented me from doing more than twitching. They rubbed against my skin, chafing it.

"I think they might." Charles looked at the wall as he spoke, as if afraid to meet my eyes. "I wasn't completely sold on this whole eating each other idea. It seems to me that if we start doing that, then we're no different than the zombies."

"Then…why?"

"Why did I go along with it?" He shrugged. "Because if I hadn't, I was afraid they'd turn on me instead. It wasn't anything personal, Pete. I've got nothing against you. But you've basically been a loner. You hide out in the movie room all day. You don't seem to understand the pull Chuck has over everyone else. Some of them are afraid of him, but a lot of the others have bought into his bullshit. I don't get it. He's not exactly charismatic or anything."

"Al…" I spat blood. "Alpha male."

"Yeah, you might be right. That's probably it. Anyway, that's why I'm going along with Chuck's plan."

"Because you're a coward?"

Charles visibly stiffened. "You don't know anything about me, Pete."

"I know that you're afraid of getting your fucking ass kicked."

"Is that what you think?" He glowered at me. "When I first lived in Philadelphia, I moved there to go to film school, but I ended up playing in a hardcore punk band and running a club called House of Conflict. You ever hear of it?"

I shook my head.

"It was basically a big warehouse. I lived on the block with the other show warehouses and we had a good neighbor policy. We looked after each other, our block and the shows. We all had keys to each other's places. My place was right next to the legendary Stalag 13. We had better bathrooms and a working washing machine, but Stalag had a skateboard ramp that went from the roof through the backyard. We used to skate on it. I helped bring bands like Unholy Grave, Vitamin X, and Cripple Bastards to play in Philly."

"And that proves you're not a pussy?"

"No. But I remember this one night, after a show at the Stalag. Some friends and I were riding our bicycles to the convenience store on 38th and Walnut, when this drunken asshole almost runs us over. He had to stop at the red light, and I jumped on the hood of his car while my friends tried to flip it over. When they couldn't do it, the three of us dragged him out of the car and beat his ass right there in the street. I'd lost friends to drunken driving, you know? I'm not afraid of a fight. I got into it with a bunch of Nazi skinheads at a show, once. They were fucking with this black kid and his white girlfriend. It was me against them—five on one, but I never thought twice about it. And believe me, I got in a few good licks before I went down."

"What's your point?"

Charles sighed. "My point is that for a scrawny ex-punk with glasses, I can hold my own when I have to. I won't back down from a fight. Although I prefer when people just do the right thing. It seems so simple."

"So then do the right thing, Charles. Let me go."

"No way. Out of the question."

"Why not?"

"Because you're insane, Pete. Do you realize what you've done?" He gestured at Jim, George, Clyde, Ritchie and Mike. "You *butchered* them!"

"They would have done the same to me."

Charles shook his head. "No. Not like this. We were going to drug you. You would have just gone to sleep, nice and peaceful. But this…what you did to Drew and Dave…you burned them alive."

"They shouldn't have gotten in my way."

"Drew was your friend."

"Was is the operative word there. A real friend doesn't sell you out to a bunch of cannibalistic crazies."

Charles paused for a moment, as if mulling over my words. When he spoke again, his voice was quiet.

"Maybe we are crazy, but you're crazy, too. You're a bad kind of crazy, Pete. There's no way I'm letting you go."

"Then stuff your goddamn speeches about doing the right thing."

"I'm in a hard spot, Pete. We all are. Before Hamelin's Revenge, I had a deep respect for people and humanity and everything that we could be. I still feel that way, although it's doubtful we'll rise up to our full potential anytime soon. But when this is all over, we're going to need leaders. We're going to need people to take charge and help rebuild civilization. It's my responsibility to do better, to be better, to be the best of humanity—and hopefully we're all part of something bigger."

"So you'll go along with Chuck just so you can stay alive long enough to get out of here and save the world?"

"If I have to, yes. And to stay alive for Carolyn."

"Who's that?"

Charles smiled. "Carolyn Sheffield. She was this hot goth

chick back in the day. To be honest, I never thought much of her until this one day when we went record shopping at Smash! in DC, and she bought a copy of Minor Threat's *Out of Step* on vinyl. We had this long, involved conversation about how the mixes on the album were better than the mixes on the compact disc. I couldn't believe this hot girl and I were talking about the mixes of a straight edge hardcore band's album, you know? I told her that I loved her. And I still do. Being stuck down here—it's taught me what's important. Somewhere along the line, I quit taking chances. I got used to working fourteen hour days and taking care of the people who rely on me and trying to make my father proud. He was a retired brigadier general. I would never let him down and nothing makes me happier than to make him proud of me. Sure, I had a mohawk until I started balding, but it was important to me that people take me seriously and believe in me. And that's a fucking hard thing to do, but while I was focused on all of those things, I stopped doing things just for me. So when we get out of here—and eventually, I believe we'll get out of here—I'm going to go find Carolyn."

I laughed. "Now who's crazy? You don't even know if she's alive, man."

"She's alive. And when I show up, she's going to play that Minor Threat record, and kiss me, and all of this will have been worth it."

At that moment, I realized that Charles had snapped. Maybe it was starvation-induced delirium, or maybe he had cabin fever from being locked up down here for too long, but he was obviously out of touch with reality. Slowly, I flexed my arms again, trying to loosen my bonds. Then I heard Alyssa. She sounded farther away.

"Pete..."

"I'm coming," I muttered. "Just hang on."

"What's that?" Frowning, Charles stared down at me.

"Nothing," I said. "I was just thinking about my wife."

"I didn't know you were married. You don't have a ring on your finger."

"Maybe not. But I am married. And when this is over, I'm

going to make it right with her. I'm going to do better. You can help, Charles. We can help each other. You let me go, so that I can find Alyssa, and I'll help you find Carolyn."

"I wish I could." His tone was wistful and apologetic. "Seriously, I do. But you're sick, Pete. I know you don't see it, but you are. I can't let you go."

"So, what are you going to do?"

"I'm going to go back downstairs and let Chuck know that I captured you. When I left, he was holed up in the lunchroom with Emma, Nicole, and Susan. I think he wants them for himself. Damonte and Phillips were standing guard. I imagine they won't be very happy when I tell them what you've done."

"But don't you see? We've got enough now to last us all year! Jim and George said you had a plan to rig something up in the incinerator room to smoke the bodies. Between that and the refrigerator, the meat will be okay. You guys don't have to kill me now."

"That's Chuck's call," Charles said. "But to be honest, I can't see keeping you alive. Not after all of this. Not after what you did to Drew and Dave."

"Are they alive?"

"Dave still was, when I left, but I don't think he will be for much longer. His skin…" Charles closed his eyes and shuddered. Then he opened his eyes again. I saw that they were wet.

"What about Drew?"

"Drew didn't make it."

"Good."

"That doesn't bother you? He was your friend."

"Fuck him. Fuck all of you. Go get your cronies. Go crawling back to Chuck like a good little boy. Your father would be ashamed of you."

He stood up so quickly that I flinched. Charles glared at me, his hands curling into fists. He trembled with anger, and a muscle twitched in his cheek. I cringed, expecting him to kick me, but then he relaxed his posture. Smiling, he calmly stepped over me and walked down the corridor.

"Go on," I yelled. "Go find Chuck. And when you do, I

want you to tell him something. Tell him that I'm going to kill every one of you motherfuckers before this is over!"

My shouts echoed down the hall. Ignoring them, Charles headed toward the power plant. I twisted and flopped, trying to get free of the wires, but they held fast. Charles disappeared through the door, leaving me alone in the corridor. I wiggled to one side and then the other, pulling my legs up to my chest and arching my back. Some of the tension in my bonds eased, but I still couldn't get free. Frustrated, I rolled toward the wall.

"Alyssa? Help me."

"I can't. You have to do it yourself. If you want me back, then you have to prove yourself to me, Pete. You have to prove that you're worthy. Find me."

"Hold that thought."

Gasping for breath, I paused when I reached the wall. In my struggles, I had rolled through a half-congealed puddle of Clyde's blood. It smeared over my clothes and skin and got into my mouth and eyes and nostrils—but more importantly, it got beneath the wires, as well. After some difficulty, I was able to sit up, and when I did, I was surprised to find that my bonds were much looser. I still couldn't free myself, but they were no longer so constricting. Pushing my back against the wall, I struggled to stand up. It was harder than I would have thought. I was weak and groggy and my head and mouth still hurt, not to mention that I was doing it without the aid of my arms. Eventually, though, I got myself upright. I stood there, leaning on the wall for support, and swayed back and forth. I experimented with my arms and shoulders and found that I could now stretch them about an inch from my sides. Still not enough to get free, but enough that I had a renewed sense of hope.

"Thanks for your help, Clyde. I really appreciate it."

I turned away from him and closed my eyes, waiting for the dizzy spell to pass. I don't know how much time went by. Maybe a minute. Maybe five. I think I might have lost consciousness for a bit. My eyes snapped open when I heard a faint skittering noise at my feet. A rat hurried by, running toward the skids. I was immediately reminded of Dude, my pet hooded rat from when I was in college. I hadn't thought of Dude in years. Alyssa had made me get rid of him when we moved in together. I'd taken him to my parent's house, and they'd looked after him until he died. I used to tell myself he died of old age, rather than a broken heart over the fact that his owner had given him up.

"Hey," I whispered. "Dude? Is that really you?"

The rat stopped, stood up on its hind legs, and stared at me. It tilted its head to the side and twitched its long whiskers. I wondered where it had come from. In all my time working for the hotel, I'd never seen a rat or a mouse in the bunker. Had it been here all along, or had it somehow found a way inside the supposedly impregnable walls? I panicked for a moment, wondering if it was infected with Hamelin's Revenge, but it didn't look dead. Indeed, it looked very much alive—and well fed, too. Its belly was round and soft and had a cute little spot of white fur, just like Dude had when he was alive.

"Dude? Hold on a second. You can't be here. You're dead."

The rat squeaked in response.

"Don't give me that. Even if you're not Dude, you could pass for his twin."

The rat squeaked again. It sounded agitated.

"Better get out of here," I said. "These people are crazy. They'll eat you if they find you."

As if heeding my warning, the rat dropped back down on all fours and scurried under the skids. I watched its tail vanish from sight, and then it was gone, like it had never been there. Maybe it wasn't. I considered that maybe it had been a hallucination brought on by starvation and the beatings I'd taken. If it had been real, and it had come from outside, then I needed to find out how. If a live rat could get into the bunker, then a zombie rat could do the same.

My stomach growled again.

"Wait," I called. "Come back, Dude!"

The rat didn't return. The corridor was quiet again. I closed my eyes and wept silently.

Once my dizziness had subsided, I stumbled over to the forklift. Ritchie was dangling there, impaled from the

97

upraised forks. I stared into his dead, glazed eyes. Then I crouched down and placed my head and shoulders against his chest. Grunting, I pushed him backward. It was a difficult task. His insides stuck to the forks and left a gory trail in his body's wake. The stench was terrible. The squelching sounds were even worse. I turned away, took a deep breath, and then renewed my efforts, pushing him to the edge of the forks. After a final, determined nudge, Ritchie's corpse dropped to the floor. I maneuvered between the forks and the blast door, and then positioned myself so that the tip of the forks caught the wires behind my back. I wriggled back and forth, driving it deeper. The cold steel slipped under my shirt, and the tension on the wires increased. Then I took a deep breath and began sliding back and forth. The wires rubbed against my chest and arms, digging deep. If I hadn't been wearing a shirt, I'm sure they would have cut me. The pain was incredible. Just when I thought I wouldn't be able to take it anymore, I felt the wires go slack. Gasping, I managed to slip free of the bonds. My skin was chafed and my shirt was torn in places, but I was free.

I paused long enough to catch my breath and work some of the kinks out of my aching muscles. My mouth still hurt, but the pain in my head had subsided. Then I walked over to the skids, got down on my hands and knees, and peered beneath them. It was dark under the slats, and I couldn't see or hear anything. There wasn't even any rat droppings. Dude had always had a habit of pooping on my shoulder when I carried him around. I edged closer, lying my cheek on the cold concrete floor.

"Dude? Was that *really* you? Are you under there? Come here, ratty. Come here, Dude..."

I lay there for another minute, relishing the coolness against my cheek. Then I stood up again and groaned at the pain. I scooped up the wires Charles had tied me with, and then took off in pursuit of him. I glanced up at the closed circuit security monitor as I ran. The dead were still out there, milling about. They were much more restless than the dead inside with me. I preferred the latter.

I saw no more rats as I ran.

I caught up with Charles just as he was finishing moving the toolbox blocking the door inside the power plant. He didn't know I was there until it was too late. As he grabbed the door handle, I hurried up behind him and looped the coils of wire around his throat. Then I jerked them hard. He made a choking sound, but I could barely hear him over the generators. He tried to throw himself forward but only succeeded in strangling himself even more. Before he could break free, I turned around, hunched over, and pulled the wires over my shoulder. The lengths bit into my hands, but I ignored the pain and discomfort and yanked harder. Charles kicked and thrashed, but I remained upright and my grip didn't slacken. Eventually, his movements weakened, and then stopped altogether. He twitched sporadically a few more times, almost like aftershocks. I waited another full minute before finally letting go of the wires. Charles fell to the floor, dead.

"Six more to go."

I flexed my hands. The wires had cut into both of them, drawing thin lines of blood. I wiped them on my pants, adding to the gore already there.

"Hurry, Pete...Find me...Kill them all and find me..."

"Oh, I plan on it, baby. Don't you worry about that." Following Alyssa's insistent urging, I opened the door and entered the stairwell. "Ready or not, here I come."

EIGHT

The stairwell still smelled like roasted meat. The aroma hung heavy in the air, and my stomach growled even louder. The hunger pains were just that—pain. It physically hurt me to be so famished. I'd felt them early on, in the long days when we'd first run out of food. But after a while, they had stopped, replaced with the constant fatigue we'd all suffered. Now the hunger pains were back. It felt like somebody was stabbing my stomach with knives. Maybe it was all psychological. Maybe they were just induced by the aroma, but my stomach muscles contracted and I groaned, shivering with both desire and pain.

Flecks of burned flesh stuck to some of the stairs, charred almost to ash, like the blackened remnants you'd find at the bottom of your backyard grill at the end of summer. Some of the skin crunched beneath my feet, crumbling to dust. There was a smeared red, pink and black handprint on one wall, and some scraps of burned clothing on the landing. Strips of charred skin also dangled from the handrails. Powdery ash floated in the air, and the ceiling and walls had sooty patches on them from the smoke. I found one of Drew's shoes lying on the landing. It was burned black. The leather had cracked and the soles had melted onto the floor. I prodded it with my foot, but the shoe was stuck fast.

"Serves you right, Drew. You backstabbing motherfucker."

Even though I'd whispered, my voice echoed in the stairwell. The effect was strange and distorted. It sounded like multiple voices all hissing at the same time. Then they all coalesced into Alyssa's voice.

"You have to be careful from this point on, Peter. They'll be waiting for you."

"You think I don't know that? I'm not crazy, Alyssa."

"I didn't say you were. But you're doing what you've always done—charging ahead without thinking about the consequences. You always think with your heart and your gut. Never your head. You can't just rush in there. You're still outnumbered."

"Only six to one, though. The odds keep getting better. Reckon I can even them some more before I'm done."

"You always were cocky."

"You used to like that about me."

"It got old, after a while."

"Is that what happened to us?"

"You know what happened to us, Peter."

"Yeah. Sometimes I think I do. Sometimes I see it clear as day. Other times, it all seems so silly. All of those things that were important. All of those things I couldn't live with. They don't seem as clear anymore. Sometimes I can feel the guilt and other times I can't. I don't know which is worse."

"Your mind does whatever it has to do to cope. But that's always been your way."

"How is it I can hear you, Alyssa?"

"Why do you ask?"

"Because I want to turn you off. I don't need this shit right now. I'm a little preoccupied with trying to stay alive and I don't feel like being lectured by my ex-wife."

"The truth hurts, doesn't it, Peter? If you want me back, then you're going to have to face up to some of these things. As for how you can hear me, I think you know the answer to that."

I nodded. "Yeah, I think I do, too. I've been thinking about it. The only thing that makes sense is that you're dead. You died of natural causes, and didn't become a zombie. Instead, you became a ghost. Just like the ghost of the little girl who supposedly haunts the restroom by the blast door. You're a spirit. Am I right?"

"You'll just have to wait and see…"

"You're a ghost," I repeated. "You have to be. That's the only way you could have gotten inside here. You and Dude. Dude died. I know that. He died long before any of this shit began, but I swear to God that I just saw him back there. And I'm hearing you. That can only mean one thing. You're both ghosts. Right?"

There was silence.

"Okay," I continued, "if you can't tell me that, then lets talk about something else. Is this bunker really haunted? I mean, other than by you? Is there really a little girl in the bathroom upstairs? I've always wondered about that. People have reported seeing her ghost from time to time. Is she really there? Is the bunker really haunted?"

Alyssa didn't respond. I paused, waiting for a reply, but I could no longer feel her presence. She'd gone again.

I fumbled through my pockets. My fingertips brushed over Jeff's wooden token, and then the pocketknife. I searched the stairs until I found my trusty and bloodstained screwdriver lying where Drew had dropped it. Then I continued downward. I had nothing against the pocketknife. It was a fine and serviceable weapon, as far as blades were concerned, but I preferred the screwdriver. We'd been through a lot together, that screwdriver and me, and it had served me well. It was one of the few friends I had down here.

I stopped at the bottom of the stairwell, remembering what had happened the last time I'd pushed the door open. Just like before, they could be waiting on the other side for me. I paused, considering my options. I was tempted to go back upstairs and climb down the incinerator chute, but decided that was just as risky. I wouldn't be able to mask my sound in the incinerator chute the way I could in the stairwell with the noise of the power plant's generators droning on in the background. Plus, Chuck and the others could have gotten smart and blocked off the chute. If so, I could end up trapped inside, especially if somebody snuck upstairs while I was inside it and blockaded the other end of the chute, as well. I imagined what would happen next in that scenario—Chuck instructing them to fire up the incinerator, and me scrabbling at the walls like a frantic gerbil, praying to die of smoke inhalation before I cooked to death.

Nervous, I took a few steps backward, and then reached

forward with the screwdriver. Using the tip, I prodded the door open and then dropped down into a crouch, preparing myself for someone to charge through. I was convinced they would. Instead, nothing happened. The door swung shut again. I held my breath and waited, but nobody came. After a few minutes had passed, my muscles began to knot and hurt, so I stood up again and cautiously approached the closed door. I put my ear to it, but heard nothing. Taking another deep breath, I inched it open and peered out into the hall. It seemed empty, at least from my limited point of view. I heard voices, but they were distant and muffled. After listening a little longer, I determined that they were coming from the dining room at the far end of the hall.

I eased the door open wider and stuck my head outside. Carefully looking both ways, I saw that the doors to the dining room were closed and confirmed that the hallway was indeed deserted. Since that could change at any moment, I moved quickly, slipping out into the corridor and then eased the door shut behind me. The conversation from the dining room seemed to grow louder. I told myself it was just my imagination. Then I crossed the hall and tried the doorknob to the library. It was unlocked, and the lights were out inside the room. I hurried inside and shut the door behind me.

The library was a relatively small room, but all four of its walls were lined with floor-to-ceiling bookshelves. They'd been built right into the wall. When the bunker had been operational, the government had kept it fully stocked and updated with everything from medical textbooks to classic literature to the latest mid-list paperbacks or hardcover bestsellers. After the bunker was deactivated and sold to the hotel, the staff had kept the books intact, as part of the overall museum experience. Unfortunately, we'd had to get rid of most of them a few years ago after a silverfish infestation. Now the shelves were mostly bare. There were a few dozen Readers Digest condensed editions that somebody had bought for a quarter apiece at a local flea market, along with various outdated magazines and newspapers. My fellow survivors had added to it after our arrival, but their contributions amounted to nothing more than a Robert Randisi western paperback with its cover stripped off, a self-help pamphlet on the wonders of colon-cleansing, and some bullshit teeny-bopper book about vampire cheerleaders in love with werewolf football players. Most of us hadn't had time to grab our belongings before fleeing below. Several of the survivors had electronic book readers in their purses, or Kindle apps on their cell phones, but those had been worthless without the chargers, all of which had been left behind in their vehicles or hotel rooms. I remembered how proud Krantz had been in our first few days of the siege. He'd complained about the bunker's selection of movies and the general lack of entertainment choices, as if he was on vacation or something, but he'd gloated over his e-book reader and the fact that it held over two-thousand books. He'd assured us that he wouldn't be bored, and that it sucked for everyone else, because he wouldn't be sharing. Of course, that two-thousand book library of his was gone now, eradicated by something as simple as a dead battery. That had always been the inherent danger of the digital age. Once a civilization's culture became electronic, that culture lasted only as long as the power was on. Archeologists could dig up ancient Rome and find statues and coins and scrolls, but a thousand years from now, what would they make of those dead little handheld gadgets we'd coveted so much?

I thought of my own books, most of which had been boxed up and put in storage or sold for cash after my divorce from Alyssa. There hadn't been enough room for them in my new apartment, and I'd had to sell some of the rarer and more collectible ones to pay the lawyer. I wished I had them now. At that moment, I'd have given anything to have them there with me. To smell them and hold them. Feel the weight of them in my hands and hear the pages turn. Before the zombies, there had been nothing like holding a physical book in my hands. Now, in this post-apocalyptic setting, that feeling would be magnified a hundred times, simply because it was a connection to a world and a civilization that was no more—and might not ever be again. My thoughts turned back to the archeologists. If humanity survived the zombie plaque and somehow rebuilt itself, would archeologists a thousand years from now discover the works of Stephen King and Tom Clancy and Nora Roberts and Nicholas Sparks, and if so, would the people of that era look upon those works as we did the writings of Homer and Byron and Shakespeare? It was a nice thought. I smiled, and immediately wished I hadn't. Doing so made my face hurt.

The overhead lights were turned off and the only illumination in the library was the soothing red of the emergency light, which always remained on in case of a fire or power outage. I stared at the soft glow. It was alluringly relaxing—a pleasant enough diversion from all the blood and violence and pain. The light did not judge. It did not weigh me. It didn't see me as a source of hurt or humiliation. Most importantly, it did not want to eat me. I kept staring, and my eyes felt itchy and heavy. I stifled a yawn and fought to stay awake and alert. Despite my very real and constant peril, the adrenalin was retreating in my body. Combined with the hunger and the beatings I'd taken, it left me feeling both nauseous and exhausted. I wanted nothing more than to lie down and sleep. Well, that's not entirely true. What I wanted more than anything was to eat, but after I'd gorged myself, a nap would be just fine. I'd sleep right here under the lights, bathed in their warmth.

"You can't sleep now," Alyssa said. *"They'll find you if you do. Fall asleep now and you'll never wake up."*

I chuckled. "The way I feel right now? That wouldn't be such a bad thing. Besides, if I don't wake up, then I can be with you. We'll both be ghosts. We can finally be together again."

"We will be together again," Alyssa promised. *"You just have to find me first."*

"I'm trying."

"Then you have to try harder. Do whatever you have to do to survive, and then find me."

I was getting pretty frustrated with Alyssa's riddles and hide-and-seek games, and was just opening my mouth to tell her so when I heard footsteps in the hall outside. My fatigue vanished, replaced with a new surge of panic. My pulse began to pound again, drowning out Alyssa's voice. I glanced around, frantically looking for a place to hide. My options were limited. The library had no nooks or crannies. Other than the bookshelves, the room held only a few long tables, a half dozen metal folding chairs, and an empty newspaper display rack. When the bunker had been active, the rack would have held current newspapers from various cities across the country. The government had changed the papers weekly—our tax dollars at work. The newspapers hung from long, grooved wooden poles that looked almost like swords. Other than these, the only other things in the library were a few small plaques that were affixed to the wall and one of the shelves. Each one gave visitors information about the library in addition to the tour guide's usual spiel.

I ducked down beneath one of the tables and held my breath. The footsteps halted right outside the library door. Then there was silence. I waited for what seemed like minutes before whoever was outside slowly moved on again. Moments later, I heard the dining room doors bang open and shut.

Breathing a sigh of relief, I crawled out from under the table and stood up. I must have done so too quickly, because my dizziness returned. I reached out and grabbed the table and waited for it to pass. My vision narrowed, as if I was looking down a tunnel, and my ears began to ring again. I bowed my head, closed my eyes and focused on breathing through my nose with short, measured breaths. I sat down on the floor and waited for the spell to pass. This time, it took a lot longer for my senses to return to normal, and even when they did, I still had a slight twinge of vertigo. It got worse every time I breathed through my nose, as if my sinuses and ears were blocked. I tried moving my jaw back and forth to ease the sensation, but it hurt too much to keep doing, and I stopped.

"Blood sugar," I whispered. "Starvation. Hunger. All the physical exertion and damage I've taken today. Exhaustion. Pain. It's a wonder I'm still awake at all. I need to keep moving. I am a shark."

"Quiet," Alyssa scolded. *"You're talking out loud. Someone will hear you."*

"I don't care anymore," I said. "Let them hear me. Let them all come. I'm sick and tired of this shit. All I want to do is sleep, but they won't leave me the fuck alone."

"You're talking funny. Listen to yourself, Pete. Your speech is slurred, and you're sitting there weaving back and forth like a drunk on a barstool. If they catch you in here, they'll kill you, and then you'll never find me."

"You're right." Sighing, I stood up slowly. My muscles ached in protest. "I'm sorry. I'm sorry for everything. I'm sorry that I lied to you and that I hurt you. I'm sorry about Hannah and I'm sorry that—"

Footsteps sounded down the outside corridor again. They were faster than before. I crawled beneath the table just as they stopped in front of the door. I hoped that Alyssa wouldn't chose that moment to say anything, and luckily, she didn't. Seconds later, the library door opened. It was hard to see from my vantage point under the table, but I saw one pair of feet and jeans-clad legs standing in the doorway, bathed in the red glow of the emergency light. I held my breath and didn't move. I was afraid to even pull out my razor knife or screwdriver. Any movement, no matter how subtle or slow, might give my location away. Instead, I waited. The person stepped into the room and slowly crossed the floor. I could hear their breathing from underneath the table. It was loud and rapid. They stopped just a few feet from my hiding place and stood still. I could tell by the direction their feet were pointing in that the intruder was facing in my direction. I tensed, preparing myself to scramble out from under the table and attack.

The intruder lowered one hand, letting it rest beside their hip. Their fingers twitched, as if they were nervous. I could tell by the fingernails that it was Nicole. I'd know those fingernails anywhere. I remembered admiring them back when we'd first come underground. They were long and well-kept and lacquered with purple nail polish with little specks of glitter in it. I'd thought them exotic—not the kind of thing you normally saw in West Virginia. The same could be said of her body jewelry and multiple piercings. She had silver studs or tiny gems not just in her ears, but in her nose, eyebrows, and lips, as well. She'd told me once that her nipples, belly button, labia and clitoris were pierced, too, but had gently rebuffed my efforts to verify this. I'd been disappointed, but not at all surprised. The only gold that Nicole wore was her wedding ring, and she talked about her little boy and her partner all the time. I think she'd grown accustomed to the idea that they were gone, but her grief hadn't let her move on. Maybe she would have, in time. Maybe she'd have moved on with me. And maybe I would have let her—if she hadn't been one of the fuckers trying to eat me. Now those fingernails were chipped and faded, and the glitter had long since worn away. So had any emotion or sympathy I'd felt for her.

Nicole stood there, still as a statue, and I noticed that there was something in her other hand. I had to look twice, certain that the emergency lighting was playing tricks on my eyes. She was clutching an aerosol can of industrial solvent—the kind used for loosening rusted bolts or lubricating machine gears. The cap was off and a small, plastic straw was sticking out of the nozzle. Her fingers were wrapped tightly around the canister, and her thumb remained on top of the nozzle at all times. Her hand was still trembling slightly, and the can jostled against her thigh. When I looked closer, I saw that her legs were shaking, too.

She's terrified, I thought. *All I've got to do is wait for her to turn around, and then ...*

I eased my hand behind my back, slowly reaching for the razor knife.

"Hello?"

I held my breath.

"Hello?"

Nicole's voice sounded very small and afraid. I stopped moving, and waited. After a moment, she spoke again. This time, she whispered.

"Pete? Are you there? It's me. Nicole. If you're in here, just listen, okay? I don't want to hurt you. I don't want any part of this. Not anymore. I'm sorry that I went along with it. I don't know why I did. You were always really sweet to me. I guess I was just scared, and I didn't want the others to turn on me instead. I know that sounds terrible, but it's the truth. I'm sorry."

I have to admit, I was moved by the sincerity in her voice. Yet still I hesitated. A part of me wanted to call out to her, to let her know that it was okay and that she had nothing to fear from me, but a bigger part of me remembered my betrayal at Drew's hands. This could be another trick—some scheme devised by Chuck and the others to lull me into a false sense of security, and then, when I came out of hiding—straight into the refrigerator I'd go, chopped and butchered like a side of beef. Instead of coming out, I waited. My muscles began to cramp from sitting still for so long, but at least my dizziness had finally passed. My headache throbbed in time with my pulse.

"Pete? Are you there?" She sighed, and then her voice grew louder. "Oh, screw this. I'm being silly. He's probably still upstairs. Or dead."

A severe cramp shot through my calf. I bit my lip to keep from crying out, but Nicole must have heard my intake of breath, because she gasped and took a step backward.

"Pete? Is that you? Did you hear what I—"

"Nicole?" Another pair of legs appeared in the doorway. I couldn't see their owner, but I knew that it was Damonte by the sound of his voice. "Anybody in there?"

She hesitated before answering. "No, I thought I heard something, but it's empty."

"You sure?"

"Yeah."

"What's up with the can?"

"I've got a cigarette lighter," Nicole said. "If I came across Pete, and he wouldn't listen to reason, then I figured I could make a blowtorch out of it."

"How do you do that?"

"Didn't you ever do that as a kid?"

"Hell, no. My mother would have beat my ass. How does it work?"

"It's easy. You just press down on the nozzle and hold the flame into the stream. You just have to be careful not to get the lighter too close to the can or it will blow back on you."

109

Damonte grunted in appreciation. "Check you out. You've gone all Rambo and shit."

"Well, we've got to make due, don't we? It's not like we have any guns."

"No, I guess it isn't. I wish to hell we did. I'd feel a lot better with a gun in my hand, given what's going on. Speaking of which, nobody has come down from upstairs yet. I set a trap around the stairwell door just now. Put some glass bottles and aluminum cans and stuff around the door. If he comes through, we'll hear him. I locked the door, too, so he'll have to make even more noise if he tries to get in."

"Do you think the others are dead?"

"The one's upstairs? I don't know. Like I said, they're not back yet. Maybe they've got him cornered and are waiting him out. Maybe they captured him and are just taking their time coming back. Or maybe...what you said. In any case, I figure better safe than sorry. I locked the incinerator door, too. Just in case Pete tries to come down that way. I figured that makes more sense than having Phillips and I walk around down here, waiting for Pete to show."

"Yeah," Nicole said, "that didn't make a lot of sense. And Chuck didn't seem too happy when I told him so."

"Speaking of which, Chuck told me to tell you that he wants you to go back to the dining room. He's already in there. Emma is in there with him."

"What about Susan?"

"She's hiding out in one of the dorm rooms. He sent Phillips to find her and bring her back to the dining room, too. Chuck wants all three of you in there with him."

"I don't care what Chuck wants. You see what's happening here, don't you, Damonte? We're all going crazy—Chuck worst of all. I know exactly why he wants us to stay in there with him."

"Yeah, well I ain't too crazy about it, either. Like I said, he wants me and Phillips to stay out here and patrol the hallways, waiting for Pete to show up. How do you think I feel about that?"

"Not too good, I guess."

"You're damned straight I don't. That's why I locked the doors and set the traps. I'd rather be in the cafeteria with you all, truth be told. You saw what Pete did to Drew and Dave. That shit was vicious. It made your little blowtorch there seem like a toy."

"Then why stay out here? Why not just ignore what Chuck tells you?"

"Because I'm more scared of Chuck than I am of Pete. So are you."

"No, I'm not."

"Yeah, Nicole. You are. Have you gotten a good look in his eyes? You're right—what you said earlier. Chuck is crazy. He's not playing around here. That's why I'm going along with things. Better not to piss him off. And besides…"

His voice trailed off. I watched Nicole walk toward him.

"Besides what?" she prompted.

"Well…I was going to say that even though he's crazy, Chuck is still right. I don't like it, but he's right about eating Pete. We're out of food. We're starving to death. We've got to do *something*."

"Yeah, but murder?"

"You voted for it, too, Nicole."

"Maybe so, but it doesn't even matter now. Chuck said we'll…he said that we can start with Drew, Dave and Krantz. And any of the others Pete might have killed. That's enough. Nobody else has to die today. If we can preserve them, that's enough to last us for months, as long as we ration the…meat… carefully. We don't have to keep up the hunt."

"Chuck doesn't agree. And to be honest, after seeing what Pete has done, I'm inclined to agree with him. Like I said, you voted for this, too. I'm thinking we made the right decision, choosing Pete the way we did. He's a fucking serial killer."

They stepped out into the hallway and Nicole closed the door behind them, muffling their voices. My temples throbbed and a muscle in my jaw twitched. I sat there until their footsteps had faded, and then I eased myself out from under the table, grimacing at the pain in my joints and muscles as I stood up again.

Damonte's final words echoed in my head. A serial killer? Is that what I was? Was that what I'd become? The post-apocalyptic wasteland's version of Ted Bundy or The Exit or Jeffrey Dahmer? Me? That was ridiculous. I mean, sure, I'd killed some people. In truth, I'd killed a lot of people. A lot. And those things weighed on my conscious the moment I allowed myself to slow down and think about it. The guilt crushed me, just like the regrets I felt over Alyssa and Hannah. But they'd left me no choice. Why couldn't they see that it had been in self-defense? Nicole was seeing it now. Why couldn't Damonte and the rest? I didn't want to kill anybody, but they'd left me no other option. If any one of them had been in my shoes, even for a moment, they'd have reacted in the same manner. None of them would have just offered themselves up as a sacrificial lamb. None of us were Jesus. We weren't going to offer up our flesh and our blood for the others to partake in, thus granting them life via our death.

A line from *Scarface* ran through my head—Al Pacino asking, "Who's the bad guy?" Well, it wasn't me. I wasn't the bad guy in this situation. Neither were the zombies, for that matter. The zombies were nothing more than window dressing. Background noise—a catalyst that got us to this point. No, the zombies didn't matter. The real bad guys were my fellow survivors. Chuck and his *people*, as he'd called them. They were the real villains.

The corridor was silent, and I was pretty sure that the coast was finally clear. As I crept toward the door, I patted my back pockets to reassure myself that my weapons were still there. The razor knife was safely tucked away, but the screwdriver was missing. I stopped and did a quick search of the library, looking under the table and carefully scanning the floor, but I couldn't find the screwdriver anywhere. I remembered picking it up in the stairwell. I'd used it to open the door. Where the hell was it now? I panicked. What if I had dropped it out in the hallway? What if Damonte and Nicole had discovered it there, and knew all along that I'd been hiding nearby? Could their entire conversation have been nothing more than an act? Could Nicole's seemingly heartfelt-apology have just been a charade, after all—an attempt to lure me out of hiding so that they could finish the job?

"Paranoia will destroy ya," I muttered.

It didn't matter. I still had the razor knife and the pocketknife, so it wasn't like I was totally defenseless. As I turned toward the door again, I glanced at the newspaper racks. On a whim, I walked over to them and grabbed one of the newspaper holders. It looked just like a wooden sword, and when I gave it a few experimental swings through the air, it felt very satisfying. I thought about snapping the tip and turning it into a spear, like I'd done with the broom handle, but decided that I liked it better this way. If I cracked somebody in the head with it, I'd certainly do some damage to them. I was confident that the wood was solid enough to break bones without the rod splintering or snapping. A memory surfaced from when I was a kid—summers spent roaming around in the little strip of woods behind my house, swinging sticks and branches like they were lightsabers. I'd liked the feeling back then, and I liked it even more now. It was comforting. Clutching the newspaper rod in my hand gave me an overwhelming sense of power, as if I were a marauding barbarian making my way through some subterranean labyrinth in search of a princess.

Which I was.

"Hang on, Alyssa."

I started to worry when she didn't respond. Even though she'd begun to annoy me, there was something safe about the familiarity of having her ever-present voice in my ear. The bunker felt emptier without it. I hoped again that she was okay.

Pushing my fears aside, I cautiously opened the door and peeked into the hall. The corridor was indeed empty. If they'd found the screwdriver and set a trap for me, then the surprise was waiting elsewhere. I noticed that there were a half dozen empty bottles and cans lined up around the stairwell door. If I'd opened the door, it would have knocked them all over. Damonte was at least telling the truth about that part, but I still wasn't completely convinced. I hurried out of the library and then noticed the screwdriver. It was lying on the floor, mere inches away from the library door. How had Damonte and

Nicole not seen it lying there? Or had they, and they'd left it there to help bait their trap? My heart rate increased, throbbing so hard in my throat that it felt like I'd swallowed an apple. Glancing around, I bent down and picked up the screwdriver. I expected to be ambushed, but nothing happened.

Just to be safe, I ducked inside the media room. I slipped the door shut behind me and leaned against it. The lights were out, but my eyes adjusted quickly. It was hard to believe that only a few hours before, I'd been sitting in here watching stoner cartoons and trying not to go crazy from hunger and cabin fever. Eisenhower still lay on his side in a congealed pool of Krantz's blood. I nodded hello at him, but he didn't nod back. I felt a sad wave of nostalgia. Other than Drew, that bronze bust of Eisenhower's head had been my closest friend and companion during these last few trying months. Many times I'd confided in him, laughed at him, and wept to him. He'd offered silent solace. He'd never spoken to me. He couldn't. Eisenhower wasn't real. I know that. I'm not crazy. But all the same, that statue meant something to me. I'd grown very attached to him, and it didn't seem right to let him lie there in a puddle of gore.

"You're a mess, Mr. President. Here. Let me give you a hand."

Kneeling, I sat my newspaper rod aside and righted Eisenhower again. His cold, hard features were sticky with blood and dirt. I tried to use my shirttail to wipe the mess away, but only succeeded in making things worse. Grunting, I picked him up and put him back on his pedestal. Then I took a step backward and studied him.

"Thanks for helping me out earlier," I whispered. "I couldn't have done it without you."

I winked, half expecting Eisenhower to wink back at me, but he didn't. The eyes stared, boring into me. The bronze features remained impassive. It may sound silly, but I began to feel uncomfortable under the statue's gaze. It felt as if Eisenhower were judging me, as if he could see inside of me and was holding me accountable for my actions.

"You don't understand," I whispered. "What other choice did I have?"

Eisenhower's silent admonishment was enough.

"I'm sorry I got you involved. I'll make it up to you once I find Alyssa. We'll restore you to a place of prominence down here."

I took another step back and my foot came down in Krantz's blood. When I withdrew my heel, it made a squelching sound. I wondered where the rest of Krantz was. Had Drew or Dave or one of the others said something about Chuck ordering Krantz to be cut up? I couldn't remember. Maybe they had, or maybe I just imagined it. For that matter, where was Dave? The last I'd heard, he was badly burned but still alive. Chances were he was in the infirmary. I decided that maybe I should check there next. Like the rest of the bunker, it was just a museum-piece now—an exhibit to give the tourists the authenticity they expected. Most of the original equipment and supplies that the government had kept here when the bunker was still active had been removed and replaced with placards and glass showcases. But the hospital beds were still there, along with a few bigger pieces of medical equipment that the hotel had elected to display. And when we'd first come down here, we'd gathered all the stuff from the first-aid kits scattered at various point throughout the bunker and stored them in the infirmary. If they were trying to save Dave, or ease his suffering until he passed, there was a good chance that was where I'd find him. Perhaps I'd find the others there, too. Or maybe they'd already eaten Dave. Maybe they'd devoured both him and Krantz and Drew, and were now saving me for dessert. Chilled Pete, served with chocolate sauce and fruit topping. Yum-yum. That's fine dining.

The longer this cat and mouse game went on, the harder it was becoming for me to think clearly. I was running on adrenalin fumes, and my hunger pangs had become a steady throb, pulsing in time with my other pains.

"Maybe I should just give up." I leaned close to Eisenhower's ear so that the others wouldn't hear me if they were lurking on the other side of the door. "Maybe I should just take my chances and try surrendering again. I mean, Nicole sounded pretty reasonable back there in the library.

Maybe she and I could try to convince the others. Get them to team-up against Chuck or something. That's got to be better than the alternatives. What's the point of going on like this? What am I turning into? Maybe Damonte was right, after all. What's the point of living if I'm no better than those things outside? Why should I keep going on?"

"I've waited so long here…"

For a split second, I thought it was Eisenhower, but it wasn't. The voice belonged to Alyssa. She was singing.

"For a reason to still carry on…"

I recognized the song right away. It was one of her favorites—'The End of The End' by Bella Morte. It's a fair statement to say that most women in West Virginia liked gospel, hip-hop, or country music (or sometimes all three) but Alyssa had always been into gothic and industrial rock. That was one of the reasons I'd fallen in love with her in the first place—not because I was particularly into that kind of music, but because she was. That's what I'd liked about her—that she was different from the other girls I met.

And I'd sullied that with my betrayal. Tears welled up in my eyes. I pushed the thought from my mind and took a deep breath.

"Alyssa? Where are you?"

"Feels like I've been living a lie, and I don't want to face it alone…"

I had a flash of memory then, so strong that I almost thought it was really happening again, and that the bunker and the zombies and the divorce and my emotional affair with Hannah had all been just a dream. Alyssa and I had driven up to Charlottesville, Virginia to see Bella Morte in concert. She'd played their music on the way up, and we had dinner and a few drinks in a quiet little pub before the show. It was a good time. In truth, I'd gone along because it made Alyssa happy. It wasn't really my kind of music or scene. The band was good, if loud, and I'd amused myself for a while by gawking at some of the Goths in the crowd. When I'd got bored with that, I'd pulled out my cell phone and updated my Facebook and Twitter accounts. Then I'd gone to the bathroom and texted Hannah. When I came back a half hour later, Alyssa was annoyed. She hadn't been able to enjoy the show because she'd been worried about me. When I didn't return right away, she'd thought something happened. I'd apologized, and lied—telling her there was a long line at the bathroom. Her glance flicked to my cell phone and then back to me. She didn't say anything. Instead, she'd simply nodded and then turned her attention back to the show.

I hadn't realized that until now. She'd suspected. Even then, she'd suspected that I was lying to her. She'd known about me and Hannah—known that it was more than a simple friendship. So why hadn't she said something at that point? Why hadn't she confronted me about it? Why did she let it drag on so long, doing incalculable damage to us all? She'd *made* me lie to her, and then allowed me to feel guilty about it. The more I thought about it, the more enraged I became. All that time I'd wasted.

"All this time that I've wasted..." Her lilting voice taunted me.

"Fuck this shit."

I stormed out of the media room, no longer caring if the others heard me or not. In fact, I hoped they would. That way, I could deal with them quickly, rather than drawing this hunt out any longer than it had to be. The only thing that mattered now was finding Alyssa and getting some answers for why she'd done the things that she'd done.

The corridor was empty. Alyssa's voice echoed softly down the hall. Before, it had been ethereal and drifting. Now, it seemed real. More solid. It stayed in one place, making it much easier for me to find her location. I glanced over my shoulder. Far down at the other end of the hall, the dining room doors remained closed. If anyone had heard me, or heard Alyssa for that matter, they weren't reacting. Of course, that didn't mean it couldn't still be a trap. Maybe Damonte or one of the others was waiting right around the corner. If so, then I had something for them.

Pausing, I moved over to the wall and stood with my back against it. Then, flattening myself out as best I could (which was easy, given then fact that I didn't have a gut to suck in anymore), I inched forward and slowly edged around the corner. This hallway was empty, too, but Alyssa's voice was nearer. My pulse pounded. As I walked, she stopped singing and began to hum instead.

"That won't help you," I whispered. "You wanted me to find you? Well, be careful what you wish for, sweetheart. You're about to get it."

The pharmacy was on my left. The door to it was closed but I could see a glow coming through the crack at the bottom of the door, indicating that the lights were on inside. I put my ear to the door and listened. After a moment, I confirmed that the humming was coming from further down the hall. I tested the knob and found it unlocked, so I nudged the door open and gave the pharmacy a quick, cursory check. It was unoccupied. I stared at all of the museum displays and placards, and wished fervently that the pharmacy still had some real drugs or medicine in it, rather than the empty bottles we used on the tour to make the surroundings look authentic, as they had when the bunker was operational. At that moment, I craved painkillers almost more than I did food. There was nothing in the room that I could use for a weapon, either. I considered smashing one of the glass display cases or mirrors, but the risk of being overheard wasn't worth it for a mere shard or sliver. My razor knife, screwdriver and newspaper rod would have to suffice. I'd killed with two of them already, and was eager to try out the latest addition, as well.

Closing the pharmacy door behind me, I continued down the hall, following the siren call of Alyssa's humming. She was doing it sporadically now, as if she'd forgotten the tune. As I neared one of the lounge areas, she started up again, but the tune sputtered into a series of choked, muffled sobs. I peeked my head through the open door and saw Alyssa kneeling on the lounge room floor. Her back was to me, and she'd buried her face in her hands. All I could see was the back of her head and her shoulders, which trembled in time with her grief. My heart broke, seeing her like that. I wanted to call out to her, wanted to run to her and take her into my arms and tell her that everything would be all right, that it would all be okay now, and that I was sorry for everything I'd done, and that we could just start over—that we could just hit the restart button and renew our relationship. We could go back to the way things were before. I desperately wanted that.

Tears ran down my bloody cheeks. I wiped them away and sniffled. If Alyssa heard me, she didn't react. Instead, she attempted to start humming again. It only lasted a few seconds before breaking into a new round of sobs. I eased the door shut behind me, not quite closing it, but enough that we would have some privacy for our reunion. The door made no sound, and the tension began to drain from my body. I stepped closer. She was so beautiful, even from behind. Even after months trapped in this bunker. I licked my lips, trying to work up the nerve to speak. Still holding the newspaper rod, I reached for her, not quite having the courage to actually touch her and make my presence known.

"I miss you." Her voice was muffled through her hands. "I miss you so much, Jose."

I froze. *Jose?* My name was Pete, or Peter as she referred to me when she was annoyed or angry. Who the fuck was Jose? I thought about all of the other men in her life—family, friends and co-workers. I'd never heard her mention a Jose before. Was he her lover? Had Alyssa been cheating on me, too? Had she let me feel guilty and forced me to lie to her in an effort to protect our relationship and maintain our happiness, while seeing somebody else all the while behind my back?

My anger returned, rushing back into my body in a flood of pent-up emotion. Tremors shot through me. My hands and feet trembled. My ears burned. The blood vessels in my forehead and neck felt like they were going to burst. So did my eyeballs. They seemed to inflate inside the sockets, and I wondered what I'd see if I looked in a mirror at that moment. Would my reflection be the monster they all said I was? I thought it might. At that moment, I was okay with being the monster. Somebody had to be.

Alyssa kept crying, whispering Jose's name over and over again. Bile burned my throat. I bit my lip to keep from screaming. My teeth sank into the fresh cuts, and the pain was exquisite. Blood ran down my chin like the juice from a fresh peach. Shivering, I went rigid. The newspaper rod slipped from my grasp and clattered to the floor, and for a brief second, time itself seemed to freeze.

Alyssa stiffened at the sound of the rod hitting the floor. Her sobs turned into a gasp. She began to turn around and I charged forward. Her eyes widened when she saw me. She tried to stand up and back away at the same time, but her feet got tangled under her. She pitched forward, and would have fallen on her face had I not been there to catch her. My arms shot out and I wrapped my hands around her throat.

"Don't worry," I whispered. "I've got you. I won't let you fall."

Alyssa stiffened in my grasp, and tried to push me away. Her movements were weak, but frantic. I tightened my grip.

"It's okay," I said, trying to soothe her. "I won't let go. I'll never let go again, sweetheart."

Whispering soothing words of comfort, I lowered her to the floor. I tried to be gentle about it, but the back of her head smacked hard against the linoleum. Alyssa's bangs slipped in front of her face. She twisted her body, thrashing and trying to get away, and as she did, her hair parted, revealing her eyes. Those same beautiful eyes that I'd stared into so many times before were now wide and bulging and filled with fear. Tiny red blood vessels filled the whites of them like spider-webs.

"Calm down, Alyssa." I squeezed harder, relishing the feel as my fingers dug deep into the flesh of her throat. "I'm not going to hurt you."

Her tongue popped out of her mouth like a glistening jack-in-the-box. Shifting my weight, I kept my grip on her neck and knelt on her stomach with both of my knees. Her entire body convulsed beneath me. She slapped the floor with her hands and kicked out behind us. She tried to raise her leg to knee me in the back, but I dug in deeper, sinking my fingernails into her flesh. Her tongue stuck out farther.

"See?" I hissed. "You wanted me to find you and I told you I would. Here I am, baby. You told me to look for you."

Alyssa punched my shoulder, but I barely felt the blow.

"This is what you wanted, right? You wanted me to look for you? Or maybe you were looking for me? Or was it other men you were looking for all along? Like when we divorced. Remember that? We signed the papers and you updated your Facebook status from the parking lot outside the lawyer's office. You'd just got done telling me that you loved me, and you were sorry it didn't work out. Then you changed your status to single, and said you were interested in dating and looking for men. Who does that, Alyssa? Who goes from 'I love you' to 'Hey, anybody on Facebook want to fuck?' that quickly? Is that how you met Jose? Did you think I wouldn't find out?"

Alyssa didn't respond. For a second, I got pissed off at her reticence, but then I realized that she probably wasn't answering because I was choking the shit out of her. I thought about letting go, but found that I couldn't. My fingers refused to obey. It felt good to squeeze her neck, so I did it some more. Her eyes grew wider. I clenched my teeth. My lips pulled back in a snarl. Saliva dripped down my chin and landed on her forehead.

"You played me, you bitch. Don't deny it. You got me to do all your dirty work. You were just as unhappy in our marriage as I was, but you didn't want to be the bad guy, so you played that passive-aggressive bullshit on me. Did it for so long, hoping I'd leave. Got me to fuck up so that you'd have an excuse to leave me. You couldn't just be honest. You had to make me be the one to lie and cheat. Fucking coward."

Alyssa struck at me again, raking her fingernails across my cheek. I gasped at the pain, and tore my head away from her reach. My cheek stung and felt warm. I put all of my weight into my knees and tightened my grip around her throat even more.

"I could have had a good thing with Hannah. She loved me. She actually fucking loved me. I didn't have all the history and baggage with her that I have with you. I hadn't lied to her. We could have made it work. But you couldn't let me have that could you, Alyssa. You took her away from me. Made me turn my back on her. And then you went right out and hooked up with this...this Jose."

Spittle flew from my lips as I said his name. Alyssa's struggles grew weaker.

"You were looking for men? Well, you found one, Alyssa. You found a man. Congratulations. Here I am, and I'll never let you go again."

I kept squeezing, even after she'd stopped moving. I didn't let go until her bladder and bowels did the same. Then I stood up quickly to avoid the mess—too quickly. The room began to spin as I gained my feet, and I reached out to steady myself and found only empty, unforgiving space. I tottered forward, stumbling, and my foot came down on Alyssa's face. I glanced down and saw that she was no longer Alyssa, but Susan.

"Oh, shit. But...but that—"

Something warm and wet tickled my neck. I reached up to touch my face and found four long claw marks running across my cheek where Alyssa had scratched it. I looked back down at Susan's left hand. Her nails were bloody. There was skin beneath them. My skin. My blood.

"But..."

I didn't recognize my own voice. It was whiny and weak. Indecisive. I hated the sound of it. I stared at Susan, confused. Then someone else called out from the hallway.

"Susan? Are you okay?"

It was Phillips. Without turning around, I recognized his voice. Unlike mine, it was strong and certain and defined. Still staring down at Susan, I reached for the screwdriver in my back pocket. The door swung open and Phillips, still speaking, stepped into the pharmacy.

"Susan? Chuck wants you to come back. I thought I heard—"

He stopped, gaping at us both. His gaze kept darting from Susan to me and then back down to her again. When he opened his mouth to shout, I charged. I clamped my left hand over his mouth, muffling his cries, and shoved him against the wall. Phillips tried to knee me in the groin, but I sidestepped his attack and thrust the screwdriver deep into his stomach. It made a farting sound as it punched through skin and fat. His eyes went wide and he took a deep breath through his nose. I felt the air rush over my fingers. Phillips tried to scream again, but I mashed my palm tighter against his mouth and stabbed him again. Phillip's moaned through my hand. His teeth grazed my skin. They felt dry, like the scales of a reptile. His skin, by contrast, was slick with sweat, and I had trouble holding him in place as I stabbed him a third time, plunging the screwdriver into his abdomen again. Phillips shuddered against me. Warmth flowed over my knuckles as I pulled the screwdriver free. Phillips' legs buckled and he started to sag forward. Grunting, I shoved him back against the wall.

"Where is she?" I asked. "Where's Alyssa? What did you guys do with her?"

He mumbled through my hand and tried to shake his head. I squeezed his mouth harder, digging my fingernails into his cheeks.

"Don't try to deny it, Phillips. I know she's here. Now where is she, you son of a bitch? Tell me."

Phillips moaned.

"I bet Chuck has her, doesn't he? The sick fuck is building himself a little post-apocalyptic underground harem. And you were going to help him, weren't you?"

Eyes-wide, Phillips tried to shake his head. I rammed the screwdriver into his stomach again. He whined. I liked the sound of it. His voice was no longer strong. He sounded like I felt.

"But now I've fucked up your plans, haven't I? Killing Susan like this. But that's your fault. You guys tricked me. Made me think she was Alyssa. Tried to pull an old switcheroo, didn't you? Well, I'm wise to you now, and I'll find her. You just watch, Phillips. You just watch."

It didn't take much effort to hold him there against the wall. I could feel the strength draining from his body as I spoke. I raised the screwdriver and twirled it in front of his face. The fluorescent lights sparkled off the crimson tip.

"You just watch."

I jammed the screwdriver into his eye. Phillips jittered

and bit through his tongue as spasms rocked his body. I stood there, relishing the feel of the tremors running through his body and into mine. They were like electrical currents. Fluid pumped from the ruined eye socket. Most of it was blood, but there was clear stuff that looked like water. His fingers drummed the wall. Then he went limp. His full weight pressed against me. If he hadn't been half-starved, he'd have probably knocked me over. I could feel his ribs rubbing up against me through the fabric of his shirt. Pushing him away, I yanked the screwdriver free. Phillips dropped to the floor, dead.

I stood there for a moment, catching my breath. I wondered if anybody else had heard our struggle, but the corridors remained quiet. I debated hiding Phillips and Susan's bodies, but I was too tired and there wasn't enough time. I had to find Alyssa and save her. I had to save us both. I had to save our marriage and make things right again. In truth, I was worried. I hadn't heard her voice since killing Susan. What if I was too late?

I stepped back out into the corridor, and passed by the incinerator room, media room, lounges, dorm rooms and the pharmacy. My nerves were taught with tension as I crept along. With each step, I expected Chuck, Emma, Nicole, or Damonte to leap out at me, brandishing clubs or knives or bricks. The overhead fluorescents reflected off the white linoleum floors like sunlight on the ocean, and made my head throb. The drab, gray concrete walls seemed to shimmer and move like heat mirages. I stared at them, convinced that the walls were breathing. Maybe the bunker was alive. Maybe I was in the belly of the beast.

My stomach growled again.

NINE

Muffled voices drifted from the dining room—a gruff male and an apologetic female. I couldn't tell what was being said, but their tone defined the conversation clearly enough. The argument was punctuated by the sound of flesh striking flesh, and then the woman's voice turned to sobs and whimpers. I ground my teeth and gripped the screwdriver so hard that my knuckles cracked. The pounding in my head grew louder. Each throb brought a fresh jolt of pain. My vision blurred again, but I kept going. That was a mistake. My knees got weak, and when I reached for the wall to support myself, I bumped my forehead against it. The wall seemed to push back. I ducked into the infirmary, intent on hiding there until this recurring dizziness had passed.

Drew, Dave and Krantz were waiting for me.

Or maybe I should say that *what was left* of Drew, Dave and Krantz were waiting for me.

I smelled the blood and shit from the moment I walked in the door. The room's ventilation system kicked in, swirling the stench around in the air. It was like walking into a wall of offal. All three corpses were laid out on metal hospital beds. One of the beds had once held a battered department store mannequin that we'd used to display during bunker tours. The mannequin now lay in the corner in a tangle of artificial limbs. Whoever had tossed it there had been more gentle with the three dead men than they had with the mannequin.

The door swung shut behind me. I stood there, still dizzy, staring down at the grisly remains. All three of them were in bad shape, but Drew was the worst of all. His blackened skin was covered with bubbles and blisters which popped and oozed under the fluorescent lights. His mouth hung open. His lips had been burned off, and his tongue was a shriveled,

125

burned thing. Even his teeth were black. They'd cracked from the heat, and looked like jagged shards jutting from his charred gums. Standing this close to them, the stench was nauseating, but that didn't stop my mouth from watering or my stomach from growling louder. The pain in my abdomen fluctuated— dull to sharp and then back to dull, but it wasn't going away. I clutched my gut, wincing at the sensation. I'd always wanted to get rid of the pot-belly I'd acquired during marriage. Now, at last, I had.

The dizzy spell passed again, and I was just getting ready to leave when I heard a strange rustling sound from out in the hall. I flattened myself against the wall to the immediate left of the door, and held my breath. A moment later, the door swung open, nearly bumping into me. When it swung shut again, I was staring at Damonte's back. He held a long butcher knife in his right hand. I assumed he must have retrieved it from the kitchen. The explanation for the rustling sound I'd heard became clear when I saw what he was wearing. He'd wrapped his body in black garbage bags from the neck down, and taped them securely with gray duct tape. They made noise with each step that he took.

Damonte walked over to the tables. His back was still to me. As he stood staring down at Krantz, he sighed heavily. His shoulders slumped.

"This is some bullshit. Why do I have to be the fucking butcher?"

Even though he was muttering to himself, his voice was thick with revulsion. He raised the knife and let the blade hover over Krantz, as if unsure of where to begin. Then he pressed it against the slick, waxen flesh covering Krantz's chest and made a hesitant cut. Shuddering, Damonte let go of the knife and turned away, retching. His back was still to me. The knife jutted from Krantz's chest. The stench of vomit now coalesced with the other odors in the room, and my stomach stopped hurting. I closed my eyes. The dizziness passed as abruptly as it had begun.

When I opened my eyes again, Damonte had turned his attention back to the task at hand. He was still turned away from me, and was hunched over, cutting with one hand and tugging on strips of flesh with the other. It took me a moment to realize that he was trying to skin Krantz—and doing a horrible job of it. Rather than pulling it away in sheets, Krantz's skin came off in hunks. I wondered if Damonte had never seen a deer butchered growing up. Had he been from around here? I could no longer remember. Fatigue and hunger had sapped not only my physical strength, but my mental alertness, as well. Damonte didn't seem to be faring much better. He kept retching and gasping, and his entire body quivered in disgust. As he yanked off another strip of flesh and laid it aside, he continued whispering to himself—nonsensical utterances of revulsion and despair, interspersed with the occasional sob.

"Just ain't right," he moaned. "Fucking bullshit. I can't take this anymore…"

I decided to put him out of his misery.

When Damonte returned to the job of butchering, I crept up behind him and clamped one hand over his mouth. At the same time, I jabbed the screwdriver into the back of his neck, just at the base of his spine. I'd seen it done in movies before, but let me tell you, it's a lot harder in real life. I had to push hard to get through the skin and cartilage, and Damonte fought, although weakly. His struggles quickly turned to jerky, spasmodic movements as the screwdriver slipped in all the way to the handle. When he stopped moving, I released him. He slumped to the floor, and the garbage bags gave one final rustle. The screwdriver still jutted from his neck. I grabbed the handle of the butcher knife instead, and yanked it free from Krantz's chest. It felt good in my hand. I bent down and stabbed Damonte a few more times with it, just to be sure he was dead, and to get a feel for the knife's weight. Then I wiped the blade and handle on Damonte's bags. Then I straightened up again and saw something that startled me so bad I nearly screamed.

A little girl stood before me, just inside the closed door. She wore a blue cotton dress with a pretty floral print pattern. The color matched that of her eyes. Her blonde hair was done up in pigtails, and her white stockings and black shoes seemed brighter and cleaner than anything else in the room. Maybe it's because they weren't coated with blood and gore, the way my own feet were. Or maybe it was because she seemed to radiate.

"I know you," I whispered. "You're the little girl who is supposed to haunt this place."

I wasn't scared. Maybe I should have been, but I wasn't. Once I'd gotten over the initial fight of unexpectedly finding someone else in the room with me after I'd just killed Damonte, I found her presence almost soothing. It was reassuring to know that I could now see a ghost, because it reconfirmed what I'd been suspecting for the last hour or so.

"I'm dead, right? I knew it. I fucking knew it! That's why I can hear Alyssa's voice in my head, and it's why I can see you. I'm dead, and this is Hell. I'm trapped here. Right?"

The apparition didn't say anything. She merely stared at me with those impossibly big blue eyes. They seemed to grow larger by the second. The illusion didn't scare me, but it did leave me unsettled.

"So if I'm dead," I continued, stepping toward her, "then none of this matters anyway, right? The things I've done here. The things we did to each other. None of it matters because none of it is real. I wonder, was I ever even down here, really? Did I die up top, when the zombies first came, and everything since then has just been another part of Hell? I mean, I know I didn't go to Heaven. Not after what I did to Alyssa. Or Hannah, even. There's no way I'd get into Heaven after hurting them both like that. So it would stand to reason that I'm in Hell. Why are you here though, I wonder? Are you in Hell, too?"

The little girl still didn't respond. Her eyes had grown even larger, shadowing out the rest of her face. As I watched, they converged into one and swallowed her nose and mouth. Her bangs now served as eyelashes. Her entire face was gone, replaced by one giant, staring pupil.

"Jesus," I whispered. "What the fuck is wrong with me? What is happening here? I just want to go home. I want things to go back to the way they were before. Please?"

The ghost pointed to the door. The gesture seemed accusatory.

"Why don't you talk? I mean, I know you don't have a

mouth anymore, but why don't you speak inside my head or something? I don't understand. What do you want me to do? What are you trying to say?"

She waggled her finger as the eyeball continued to grow, absorbing her entire head. Then she stepped aside, still pointing. I brushed past her and placed my hand against the door. When I turned to look, the girl was gone. Not even the eyeball remained.

"I'm not crazy," I said.

I'm not sure who I was talking to. Krantz, Drew, Dave and Damonte didn't respond. If they had, I wouldn't have been surprised. If this was indeed Hell, then they weren't really dead. I'd seen the proof myself. Watched it spill into the hotel. Watched it consume our world. Watched it displayed on the video monitors. There was no death. Things didn't die here. People and animals didn't die. They came back, to torment the living.

I patted my pocket and felt Jeff's wooden coin rub against my thigh. I thought of the slogan emblazoned on the token— IT IS WHAT IT IS. That was good advice. It worked for me.

I pushed the door open and strode out into the hallway. I didn't care anymore about being heard, because it didn't really matter. I wanted Chuck and Nicole and Emma to know I was coming. I wanted them to be afraid. I wanted my wife back, and they were the key to finding her. If they were fearful, then maybe this would go a lot quicker.

I shoved the dining room door open, took two steps inside, and saw Alyssa and Hannah standing against the far wall. They looked as surprised as I felt, but they also seemed terrified.

"It's okay." I held up my hand to reassure them both, realizing too late that I was still clutching the butcher knife. I lowered it again. "Hannah? I knew Alyssa was here, but are you dead, t—"

Too late, I noticed the figure looming to my left. I started to turn but Chuck lunged forward and swung one of the dining room's metal folding chairs at my head. It connected with a loud crack that deafened me for a few moments. I felt my teeth shatter and my jaw went numb. It was a sickening sensation, worse than any of the pain I'd experienced up until then. I tried to scream but only managed to squawk. My cheek felt hot and wet, and my vision dimmed.

Chuck growled, a primal, animalistic sound that had no human cadence or syllables. His face was a mask of ferocity. He lifted the chair to strike again, but I darted to the right until I was out of his reach. The girls screamed. I wanted to scream, too. Chuck didn't scream. He grunted. Raising the knife, I turned to face him. My face throbbed.

"Come on, you fucker." I don't know if he understood me or not. I could barely understand myself. It hurt to talk. Hurt to breathe. My grip on the knife tightened.

I expected Chuck to charge me, or at least growl some more, but he didn't. Instead, he stood up straight and held his ground. A crooked smile slowly broke across his face. This was the only opportunity I'd had since entering the dining room to really study him. The first thing I noticed was that he was naked. I wondered how I'd missed that fact until now. He'd drawn different symbols and doodles on his skin with what looked like black permanent marker. They seemed meaningless and random—sigils and runes, a star, a ridiculous pair of tits with a vagina beneath them (no face or body to accompany them), a crude maze with a black squiggle at the center, a cat head, a dog head, several stick figures engaged in various sex acts, and what appeared to be some kind of flag. While the effects of starvation were evident, Chuck was still in decent shape and much bigger than me. Despite losing some of his muscle mass, and despite the fact that his ribs showed through his skin just like the rest of us, I had no doubts that he was still stronger than me. If I let him get in close, he'd easily overpower me. Plus, he was obviously insane. Maybe he'd been crazy to begin with, or maybe he'd just contracted cabin fever after being cooped up for so long down here in the bunker, but whatever the cause, Chuck was absolutely bat-shit.

"You shouldn't have disobeyed me, Pete." His tone was almost sad.

"Fuck you." I spoke slowly. Each syllable was an exercise

in agony. "Who died and put you in charge?"

"I'm in charge because I was meant to be. I'm the strongest. That means I'm the leader."

"You're not a leader, Chuck." I ignored the pain. "You're a cable repairman."

"No." He shook his head. "I was a cable repairman. Now, I am something else."

"Yeah, you are. You're crazy."

"Crazy?" Laughing, Chuck edged closer to me. "Have you seen yourself lately, Pete? Crazy! Pot, meet kettle."

I opened my mouth to respond and one of my teeth fell out. Instinctively, I glanced down at it, and Chuck threw the chair at me and lunged. I jumped back. The chair hit me, but the force was lessened. Chuck followed it, fists raised. He swung at my face, probably hoping to finish what he'd already started on my jaw, but I pulled my head back and slashed at him with the knife. The blade slid across the underside of his forearm, leaving a red line through several makeshift tattoos. Chuck yanked his arm away, but made no sound. He swung again, this time with an uppercut. His fist sank into my stomach, knocking the wind from my lungs. I staggered backward, desperately trying to breathe and clutching the knife. If I let go of it now, he'd kill me in seconds.

Alyssa and Hannah both screamed. I glanced in their direction and was surprised to see that Nicole and Emma had taken their place. I tried to cry out, tried to ask where the others had gone, but all I could do was wheeze. Thick strands of bloody saliva ran from my mouth. Chuck surged toward me, ready to rain down more blows. I lashed out with the knife and he fell back, just beyond my reach.

"Give up," he said, grinning. "Give up now and I promise you I'll make it quick."

Gasping, I shook my head.

Chuck laughed. "Look at yourself, Pete. You're a mess. How long do you think you can last? Why do this to yourself? It's not like you've got anything to live for, anyway. I mean, your wife is dead by now. Not that I see why you'd care. Not after the way you fucked around on her." He paused, noticing my expression. "Oh, yeah. I heard all about that from your co-workers. People still like to gossip, even if it's the end of the world. I know your secrets, Pete. You're not the hero in this movie. I am. I'm the guy who—"

I screamed as I leaped at him—a hoarse, wounded, inarticulate cry of pure rage and grief. Blood flew from my mouth. The pain was overwhelming, but I didn't care. The things Chuck was saying hurt me far worse than shattered teeth or a possibly-broken jaw. I thrust the knife forward, not caring where I hit. The first swipe opened a cut on his bicep, but Chuck managed to dodge the next two strikes. He swung again at my stomach, but I slapped the blow away. His fist glanced off my forearm, and I lost feeling in my hand for a second.

Chuck grabbed my other wrist and squeezed, trying to force me to drop the knife. The pain was incredible. It felt like my bones were being ground together. His teeth were bared in a grimace, and his breath was hot on my face. He squeezed harder, and then grabbed my other hand. I worked up a mouthful of blood and saliva and then spat it in his face. It stank. Flinching, he reeled backward, but didn't let go. I stomped on the arch of his bare foot and he yelled. Suddenly, the pressure was gone and my arms were free again.

"Kill you," he shouted. "Kill you, you crazy fuck."

"You're the one whose crazy, Chuck."

He did something unexpected then. Instead of throwing another punch or lunging at me, he dropped to the floor and swung his leg out, kicking me hard in the knee. There was a popping noise, followed by a fresh burst of pain. My legs buckled and I dropped. I barely managed to keep my grip on the knife.

On the far end of the dining room, Nicole and Emma had turned back into Alyssa and Hannah again. Both of them cowered atop a table in the far corner, watching with horror as I fought to rescue them.

"It'll be okay," I tried to say, hoping they could understand me. "It will all—"

Chuck's heel slammed into my chin, jerking my head up

and knocking me backward. My teeth clamped down on my tongue, and my mouth filled with more blood. Something small but solid slid down my throat, and I wondered if I'd just swallowed a piece of myself. If so, it was the only thing I'd had to eat in too long a time. My stomach growled again. I lay there, sprawled on my back. The lights seemed to dim and there was a rushing sound in my ears. When I tried to sit up, I found to my dismay that I couldn't. My body didn't seem to work anymore. Worse, I'd lost the butcher knife and was now defenseless.

Chuck squatted over me, one knee on each side of my ribs, and grabbed my collar. Then he leaned over and yanked my head up off the floor until my face was only inches from his. I watched my blood run slowly down his cheeks and forehead.

"I'm not even going to bother to cook you," he said. "I'm going to eat you raw."

I shook my head. When I opened my mouth to speak, all that came out was a low wine. The room wouldn't stop spinning.

"What's that?" he asked, leaning closer still. "What did you say, Pe—"

I clamped down on his nose with my broken teeth and with every last reserve of strength, bit him as hard as I could. I can honestly say that I think it hurt me worse than it hurt him, but at that moment, I didn't care. The result was instantaneous. Chuck wriggled and shrieked as if he'd been electrocuted. Warm blood—his blood—filled my mouth, and I relished the taste. It was different from my own. He tried to pull away, but I exerted more pressure. My jaw and teeth were in agony, and the harder I bit, the more it hurt. I'd never felt anything more delightful. It was better than sex. He struggled harder, hammering me with wild, frantic blows, but I barely felt them. His blood rejuvenated me. Filled me. The pain was like the morning's first cup of coffee. I felt reborn.

Chuck gave one final, mighty heave and my teeth clacked together as his nose came off in my mouth. Screaming, Chuck toppled backward. Blood gushed from the ragged hole in his face. His hands fluttered to the wound in a futile attempt to staunch the flow. I sat up slowly, chewing the morsel, relishing the taste and feel and texture. I wanted more. As Chuck flopped around, I found my knife.

I tried to speak, tried to tell him that the first thing I'd need to do was skin him, because I didn't relish eating those magic marker tattoos. I wanted to tell him these things, but I didn't because it hurt too much to talk. Instead, I decided to just show him what I intended to do.

And then I did.

***

It is what it is. Just like it says on the wooden token.

You do whatever you have to do to survive in this place. Things are how they are. And if the situation changes, and life throws you a curveball, then you'd better well fucking adapt.

Adapt or die.

I didn't know for sure if we were alive or dead, in the bunker or in Hell, and in the days since all of that happened, I still don't know. But Alyssa and Hannah are here with me, and that's all that really matters, in the end. They screamed a lot, the first day, but they calmed down after I proved that I could provide for them. They're not hungry anymore. They won't starve. Oh, believe me, it wasn't easy, proving myself to them. They didn't want to eat at first. I had to force them. But I think they like it now. They like staying alive.

Chuck was the alpha male, but Chuck is gone. Now, I am the alpha male. That means I'm the leader. The leader of the pack. The top dog in this dog eat dog world, and as such, we ate the former top dog first. Now we've started on the others. They should last us awhile. And, eventually, when we run out of food again, I'll finally open the bunker doors and go outside in search of fresh meat. Those things out there can't hurt us. I have no fear of them.

I'm already dead.

BRIAN KEENE is the author of over twenty-five books, including *Darkness on the Edge of Town*, *Urban Gothic*, *Castaways*, *Kill Whitey*, *Dark Hollow*, *Dead Sea*, *Ghoul* and *The Rising*. He also writes comic books such as *The Last Zombie*, *Doom Patrol* and *Dead of Night: Devil Slayer*. His work has been translated into German, Spanish, Polish, Italian, French and Taiwanese. Several of his novels and stories have been developed for film, including *Ghoul* and *The Ties That Bind*. In addition to writing, Keene also oversees Maelstrom, his own small press publishing imprint specializing in collectible limited editions, via Thunderstorm Books. Keene's work has been praised in such diverse places as *The New York Times*, The History Channel, The Howard Stern Show, CNN.com, *Publisher's Weekly*, Media Bistro, *Fangoria Magazine,* and *Rue Morgue Magazine.* Keene lives in Pennsylvania. You can communicate with him online at www.briankeene.com or on Twitter at @BrianKeene

deadite press

"Urban Gothic" Brian Keene - When their car broke down in a dangerous inner-city neighborhood, Kerri and her friends thought they would find shelter inside an old, dark row home. They thought they would be safe there until help arrived. They were wrong. The residents who live down in the cellar and the tunnels beneath the city are far more dangerous than the streets outside, and they have a very special way of dealing with trespassers. Trapped in a world of darkness, populated by obscene abominations, they will have to fight back if they ever want to see the sun again.

"Jack's Magic Beans" Brian Keene - It happens in a split-second. One moment, customers are happily shopping in the Save-A-Lot grocery store. The next instant, they are transformed into bloodthirsty psychotics, interested only in slaughtering one another and committing unimaginably atrocious and frenzied acts of violent depravity. Deadite Press is proud to bring one of Brian Keene's bleakest and most violent novellas back into print once more. This edition also includes four bonus short stories.

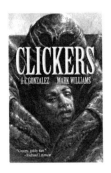

"Clickers" J. F. Gonzalez and Mark Williams- They are the Clickers, giant venomous blood-thirsty crabs from the depths of the sea. The only warning to their rampage of dismemberment and death is the terrible clicking of their claws. But these monsters aren't merely here to ravage and pillage. They are being driven onto land by fear. Something is hunting the Clickers. Something ancient and without mercy. *Clickers* is J. F. Gonzalez and Mark Williams' gore-soaked cult classic tribute to the giant monster B-movies of yesteryear.

"Clickers II" J. F. Gonzalez and Brian Keene- Thousands of Clickers swarm across the entire nation and march inland, slaughtering anyone and anything they come across. But this time the Clickers aren't blindly rushing onto land - they are being led by an intelligence older than civilization itself. A force that wants to take dry land away from the mammals. Those left alive soon realize that they must do everything and anything they can to protect humanity – no matter the cost. *This isn't war, this is extermination.*

"A Gathering of Crows" Brian Keene - Five mysterious figures are about to pay a visit to Brinkley Springs. They have existed for centuries, emerging from the shadows only to destroy. To kill. To feed. They bring terror and carnage, and leave blood and death in their wake. The only person that can prevent their rampage is ex-Amish magus Levi Stoltzfus. As the night wears on, Brinkley Springs will be quiet no longer. Screams will break the silence. But when the sun rises again, will there be anyone left alive to hear?

"Take the Long Way Home" Brian Keene - All across the world, people suddenly vanish in the blink of an eye. Gone. Steve, Charlie and Frank were just trying to get home when it happened. Trapped in the ultimate traffic jam, they watch as civilization collapses, claiming the souls of those around them. God has called his faithful home, but the invitations for Steve, Charlie and Frank got lost. Now they must set off on foot through a nightmarish post-apocalyptic landscape in search of answers. In search of God. In search of their loved ones. And in search of home.

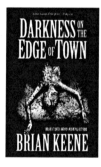

"Darkness on the Edge of Town" Brian Keene - One morning the residents of Walden, Virginia, woke up to find the rest of the world gone. Surrounding their town was a wall of inky darkness, plummeting Walden into permanent night. Nothing can get in - not light, not people, not even electricity, radio, TV, internet, food, or water. And nothing can get out. No one who dared to penetrate the mysterious barrier has ever been seen again. But for some, the darkness is not the worst of their fears.

"Tequila's Sunrise" Brian Keene - Discover the secret origins of the "drink of the gods" in this dark fantasy fable by best-selling author Brian Keene. Chalco, a young Aztec boy, feels helpless as conquering Spanish forces near his village. But when a messenger of the gods hands him a key to unlock the doors of human perception and visit unseen worlds, Chalco journeys into the mystical Labyrinth, searching for a way to defeat the invaders. He will face gods, devils, and things that are neither. But he will also learn that some doorways should never be opened and not all entrances have exits... Tequila's Sunrise.

THE VERY BEST IN CULT HORROR

deadite
press

"Urban Gothic" Brian Keene - When their car broke down in a dangerous inner-city neighborhood, Kerri and her friends thought they would find shelter inside an old, dark row home. They thought they would be safe there until help arrived. They were wrong. The residents who live down in the cellar and the tunnels beneath the city are far more dangerous than the streets outside, and they have a very special way of dealing with trespassers. Trapped in a world of darkness, populated by obscene abominations, they will have to fight back if they ever want to see the sun again.

"Ghoul" Brian Keene - There is something in the local cemetery that comes out at night. Something that is unearthing corpses and killing people. It's the summer of 1984 and Timmy and his friends are looking forward to no school, comic books, and adventure. But instead they will be fighting for their lives. The ghoul has smelled their blood and it is after them. But that's not the only monster they will face this summer . . . From award-winning horror master Brian Keene comes a novel of monsters, murder, and the loss of innocence.

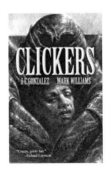

"Clickers" J. F. Gonzalez and Mark Williams- They are the Clickers, giant venomous blood-thirsty crabs from the depths of the sea. The only warning to their rampage of dismemberment and death is the terrible clicking of their claws. But these monsters aren't merely here to ravage and pillage. They are being driven onto land by fear. Something is hunting the Clickers. Something ancient and without mercy. *Clickers* is J. F. Gonzalez and Mark Williams' gore-soaked cult classic tribute to the giant monster B-movies of yesteryear.

"Clickers II" J. F. Gonzalez and Brian Keene- Thousands of Clickers swarm across the entire nation and march inland, slaughtering anyone and anything they come across. But this time the Clickers aren't blindly rushing onto land - they are being led by an intelligence older than civilization itself. A force that wants to take dry land away from the mammals. Those left alive soon realize that they must do everything and anything they can to protect humanity – no matter the cost. *This isn't war, this is extermination.*

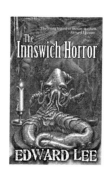

deadite
press

"Dark Hollow" Brian Keene - Eerie, piping music is heard late at night, and mysterious fires have been spotted deep in the woods. Women are vanishing without a trace overnight, leaving behind husbands and families. When up-and-coming novelist Adam Senft stumbles upon an unearthly scene, it plunges him and the entire town into an ancient nightmare. Folks say the woods in LeHorn's Hollow are haunted, but what waits there is far worse than any ghost. It has been summoned…and now it demands to be satisfied.

"The Cage" Brian Keene - For the employees of Big Bill's Home Electronics, it's just the end of another long workday—until a gunman bursts into the store and begins shooting. Now, with some of their co-workers dead, the hostages are disappearing one-by-one, and if they want to survive the night, they'll have to escape… THE CAGE.

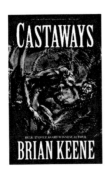

"Castaways" Brian Keene - They came to the deserted island to compete on a popular reality television show. Each one hoped to be the last to leave. Now they're just hoping to stay alive, because the island isn't deserted after all. Contestants are disappearing, but they aren't being eliminated by the game. They're being taken by the monstrous, half-human creatures that live deep in the jungle. The men will be slaughtered. The women will be kept alive as captives. Night is falling, the creatures are coming, and rescue is so far away…

"Kill Whitey" Brian Keene - In the Russian criminal underworld there is a man named Whitey. He is unstoppable and always gets what he wants. Some say he can't be hurt. Some say he can't be killed. Larry Gidson is about to find out. He is a dock worker on the run with Sondra Belov, a beautiful stripper. Whitey wants Sondra and he will torture and kill to get her. Larry, his friends, and even his cat will never be safe unless they give him Sondra – or they kill Whitey.

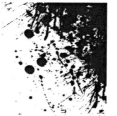

CPSIA information can be obtained at www.ICGtesting.com
Printed in the USA
BVOW021904190912

300839BV00005B/86/P

9 781621 050490